G

Solver

in

Wonderland

EE RAWLS

For my mother,
for making me laugh and helping me make this story be
the best it can be!

Madness Solver in Wonderland. Copyright © by E.E. Rawls 2021

Cover art by Curlyhair Nadia

ISBN 978-0-9985569-6-3

www.eerawls.com

Printed in the U.S.A.

First edition, May 2021

TITLES BY E.E. RAWLS

EARTHAVERSE:

~ ๑ ๑ ~

DRAEV GUARDIANS SERIES

Strayborn (1)

Dragons & Ravens (1.5)

ALTEREDVERSE:

~ ๑ ๑ ~

Portal to Eartha

Beast of the Night

Madness Solver in Wonderland

COMING SOON:

Strayblood (2)

Frost

www.eerawls.com

"When I used to read fairy tales, I fancied that kind of thing never happened, and now here I am in the middle of one!"

—Alice in Wonderland,
by Lewis Carroll

Tick-tock turns the clock
Away your lifetime flies,
Hurry before the ticking stops
And it's time to say goodbye.

Solve the case
Wonderland awaits
Don't leave behind regrets.
With all your soul
Fulfill the goal,
Peacekeeper marionette.

With pure intentions
End evil's ambitions
Let justice be dealt anew.
Unwavering resolve
As the worlds revolve
Seek and you shall find the truth.

Tick-tock turns the clock
Away your lifetime flies,
Hurry before the ticking stops
And it's time to say goodbye.

—Rhyme of the Madness Solver

❀1❀

MADNES HATTER

The air felt damp against his cheeks while he watched the last shovels of dirt fall to cover Rose's grave.

Madnes hadn't known Auntie Rose all that well. She'd been cheerful, had a smile as bright as a sunbeam, and was always busy doing something—that was all he could remember from the few times she'd visited their family.

Now, the pastor spoke a few parting words, and then the funeral gathering dispersed. People drifted off, back to their waiting steam cars, in a solemn line.

"So young...she was so young," Madnes heard an older woman saying as she wiped her eyes with a handkerchief.

"I know." His uncle comforted the woman, arm around her frail shoulders and letting her lean on him as they crossed the cemetery grass.

Madnes felt a hand touch his back and he glanced up to see his mother's eyes, still damp. "Mom, why did she die?" he asked her. It was a question that nobody seemed to have a clear answer for.

Mom brushed his carrot-red bangs back from his face; she hated bangs and the way they could hide people's expressions. "Death isn't something for you to worry about now, little Hatter. You're much too young," she told him, her gaze becoming distant and unfocused.

Madnes scratched an inch on his forehead. "I'm in high school—stop acting like I'm a kid! And anyway, that's not why I asked. I just want to know what she died of," he persisted.

But Mom's arm steered him away, walking to where Dad stood waiting at their car, and she said nothing more.

Madnes glanced back over his shoulder at the now lonely plot of upturned soil, the single black alder beside it bowing its branches with a sudden breeze.

A gray tabby cat strode over to pause at the tree. It stood up on its hind legs and bowed its head solemnly, as if in mourning. If that wasn't a strange enough sight, the cat was also wearing a peculiar vest and a bowler hat.

Madnes gaped. He blinked rapidly and looked again, making sure he wasn't just seeing things.

But the strange cat was gone.

One Year Later

Madnes Hatter pedaled his bike along the curving sidewalk atop the cliff face, overlooking a stretch of rock-and-sand beach and the sea shimmering under a late golden sun. A gust of wind blew his bangs back and threatened to snatch off his top hat; he readjusted the goggles strapped around its base.

His gaze lingered on the sunset streaked clouds, wishing he could melt into them and leave this island behind—this place that was all he'd ever known. A wide world lay just beyond the ocean channel, just waiting for him to explore...if only traveling wasn't so expensive.

His dad traveled to the mainland all the time, a place which he claimed was full of people and problems worse than their Oswick Island home—a British island in the Mediterranean Sea. He went there on business trips, and never let Madnes tag along. They didn't exactly have the best relationship.

The sidewalk led Madnes onward past the view of the beach, and soon a small, two-story building approached on his left. The large sign there read: *Designer Hats & Accessories.* Every window of the building displayed fantastic pieces of headwear, some extravagant and others utterly ridiculous. But the biggest draw of attention was the massive top hat perched on the building's roof, tilted to one side. The roof was even curved a bit to resemble a head.

'Why didn't they just build the shop out of a giant mannequin?' Madnes thought to himself.

His parents loved to stand out in society just as much as he *hated* to stand out. That's why his dad changed his last name to Mom's, Hatter, after they married. Hatter was a prestigious name in the hat-making industry.

His bike turned into the pebbled driveway. Flipping the break on, Madnes hopped off.

The door's bell jingled when he stepped inside.

"You're late, little hat." Mom glanced his way while inspecting a green, feathered piece she held up to the light.

Madnes grunted, "*Hmph.*"

"Did the book club run late?"

"*Hmph.*"

"Not very talkative today, I see."

He took out a sandwich from the fridge and headed for the backyard to eat in solitary peace. Mom made a tut-tut sound with her tongue.

His parents put all their time and energy into running this designer hat shop. Their actual home was up on the second floor, and that convenience made their work schedule become practically 24/7.

He tossed his satchel on a white chair in the backyard garden and sat down, settling his teeth into the sandwich.

An airship hummed on its journey across the sky, the balloon of its upper half reflecting the sun. Throughout the town around him, trails of steam rose above rooftops from chimneys like foggy tendrils. Steam-powered electricity was what ran the island, and it kept their population thriving.

Madnes watched a few of the tendrils from their own chimney drift idly into the sky. Oswick had rebuilt itself with the use of steam, pipes and gears, ever since the Solar Storm Wipeout that had hit Earth before Madnes was born and had wiped out every electrical grid across the globe.

He flicked off his top hat, letting it fall into his lap. Hats — he wanted more than a future of making hats like his parents. He didn't know what sort of future, but something — *anything* — different from Oswick's daily routine.

Something that would add spice to all the boring…

But tomorrow came, as tomorrows often do, and another boring day of school passed by Madnes. He carried his satchel of books down the bustling hallway at the end of classes.

"What should I do?" Harrey kept asking him as he followed after, desperation in his voice. And when Madnes wouldn't answer, he grabbed the front of his shirt, like a frantic drama king, and shook him. "What should I do?" he asked louder.

"You could stop wrinkling my shirt, for a start," said Madnes.

Harrey released him. Needing to do something with his hands, he scrubbed them over his scalp, yanking at his brown hair like a crazed rabbit. "She refused me! The love of my life refused to go out with me!" Harrey moaned. "She's killed me, I tell you, her cruel words a dagger through my heart. And now I'm bleeding internally, soon to die…"

Madnes huffed and looked away. "Can I go now?"

"You're so callous! Have a little sympathy for your dying friend, here."

"Harrey. You do this every time a girl refuses to go out with you. Give up, and do your homework for once."

"Nooo~! Heartless. You're heartless!"

Madnes exited the school doors, the atmosphere shifting from dim hallway to open daylight. He left Harrey March behind to wallow in his temporary misery. Madnes had better things to do with the rest of his day than listen to Harrey's whining and moping over his love life.

He breathed in the outdoors air. A swish of blonde off to the side caught Madnes's eye. There, waiting several paces ahead, stood Alice; she turned when she heard the door and saw them.

"Is he moping again?" she asked around a lollipop, nodding to indicate Harrey who had followed him out.

Madnes nodded. "And for the same typical reason."

She fell into step with him, both of them hurrying to leave Harrey behind as he dragged his feet at the speed of a depressed snail and moaned.

Madnes glanced to the side at his friend. Alice wasn't tall, but her eyes like large pools of sea-green had a way of captivating a person. She wore the female version of the school's brown plaid uniform and a green ribbon in her thick, yet short hair.

Alice was odd in her own way, but not nearly as bothersome as Harrey could be. In fact, he quite enjoyed her company. Together they walked from school, following the sidewalk as it led past a bustling street of steam cars and houses on one side, and the open seacoast on the other.

Alice glanced sidelong up at him. "You have a bored look on your face," she commented.

"I *am* bored."

"Every day you look like that."

"Every day I'm bored."

"Oh?" Her head tilted, blonde tresses dangling just above her shoulders. "Is this small world too boring for you, now?"

He gazed ahead. "It's always the same. Same town, same people, same problems, same future of hat-making waiting ahead of me…it gets old."

"Hmm, a land without wonder and hope is a boring place, indeed. Oswick has become that," she said.

Madnes turned his head to look at her. She flashed him a mysterious smile and then trotted away. Her house was down the nearby street. She waved the lollipop at him as she left, and he lazily waved back.

What was she getting at by saying that? He wondered.

Continuing onward, Madnes tipped his hat back to watch the sea and the shifting waters as they struck against the rocky shore below.

After walking for a while, the buildings and houses on his left were obscured by trees and a small park. He paused there and rested his elbows on the stone railing overlooking the cliff.

"A land without wonder..." he thought out loud. "I need a real wonderland then, is that it? A place that's never boring. Ha, how great it'd be to find such a place!" He said it with sarcasm, knowing it would never happen.

Seagulls cried overhead. He closed his eyes against a warm gust of air and tasted salt on his tongue.

"A wonderland..." he whispered.

"Help!"

A sudden cry came, jolting him out of his thoughts, and was followed by a loud splash.

Madnes opened his eyes and hurried to look over the rail.

Below, where the sea came up to the cliff, a small round hat bobbed in the water. Someone had fallen in!

Madnes hoisted himself over the rail, finding footholds in the cliff face's slope of rock. He fumbled his way down, then jumped, landing in the water.

He splashed about, spitting saltwater, and scanned every which way. But there was nothing to be seen anywhere except the hat.

He sucked in a breath and dived, forcing his eyes open in the saltiness.

Still, there was nothing, no one below the waves.

Madnes resurfaced and clambered up onto the rocky bank, panting. After a while, he managed to climb himself back over the rail, his palms scraped red from the effort.

Where had that cry for help come from? If it wasn't from the water, then...

"A heart that is willing to save others at your own peril. You've passed the test!" spoke a voice.

Madnes sharply turned around, but no human was in sight.

Great. Had he been cursed to hear ghost voices now? He never should have complained about being bored!

That was when a pair of paws suddenly smacked him in the face, pressing on his eyelids, and Madnes stumbled back, swatting the attacker away.

A brilliant light flashed behind his eyes and a strange sensation of energy washed through his body. He gasped and clutched at his aching eyeballs. "Ouch! What the heck…?"

Madnes blinked rapidly, massaging the pain, and wiping water away.

Before him on the stone railing sat a gray tabby cat.

It didn't seem any different than your average tabby, except that its fluffy features had been neatly smoothed, and it wore a suit and cravat on the upper half of its body. Okay, maybe it *was* different from your average tabby. Oddly different. Did ghosts normally appear as well-dressed cats?

Madnes watched in both amazement and horror as the tabby rose to stand on its hind legs and bowed with a flourishing paw in greeting, flashing him a too-big smile.

"Your vision has been awoken, Madnes Hatter," said the cat. "I've followed you these many years, waiting for the opportune time when you would be ready, and now you are! It is a heavy responsibility that lies before you."

"W-w-what…?" Madnes stuttered, unable to wrap his mind around the absurdity before him. "Talking cat? Responsibility? What crazy dream am I having?" He slapped the sides of his face, hoping to wake himself up. "What sort of ghost *are* you?"

"Ghost? I am real and alive, thank you very much." The cat tsked at him. "And neither is this a dream. You've seen me before, remember?"

Madnes thought back. The funeral, Auntie Rose, the strange tabby by the grave...

"For many generations, this gift has been granted to a member of the Hatter family. And starting today, it is *your* turn," the tabby said.

"What gift?"

Paws suddenly grabbed and turned Madnes's head around so that he was facing the park and playground behind him. It looked every bit a normal playground, just as it always did every day he passed by it. But...something felt off.

Where rocks had littered the playground border, huge red-and-purple mushrooms grew large enough to sit on. A strange bird with a head shaped like a hammer squawked and dove past a child, and the child stared about as if wondering what had stirred the air but couldn't see it.

"There's never been a bird like that in Oswick," Madnes exclaimed.

As he continued to watch, a cluster of bananas ran past him—hurrying across the lawn with a waddling stride and wearing little headbands.

"Running...bananas?"

"Ninja bananas, to be precise," the cat corrected.

Madnes rubbed at his eyes, making them water.

"It won't go away, Madnes. What you're seeing are life-forms from another world: Wonderland, as the portals link it to Earth, here in Oswick," the cat explained. "My name is Cheshire, by the way. And I'm here to train you to become the next Madness Solver!" He flashed a wide smile.

Madnes turned his head slowly toward the cat. "The...*what?*"

"Madness Solver." Cheshire shrugged as if it were obvious. "The person who works to keep the balance between worlds."

Cheshire waited, but only confusion and revulsion that a cat was talking to him showed on Madnes's face.

"You now see things that no other human here can," Cheshire continued. "Those are mushrooms back in Wonderland, but when in your world, they appear as rocks. The ninja bananas appear like regular bananas to anyone else here, but *you* can see their true form. Only you and those of Wonderland see true forms." Cheshire's paws gestured while he explained. "It's common logic that when two worlds collide there are bound to be problems and conflicts. And it's your job to solve them before anyone gets hurt." One paw rubbed his whiskered chin. "To put it another way, you are the Wonderland peacekeeper. That's who the Madness Solver is, and what you will do."

"So, when I eat a banana…" Madnes began.

"No, not every banana is alive—that's just their Earthly disguise, since they're already banana-shaped," Cheshire straightened out.

"Oh…" was all Madnes could manage to say. He stared at the tabby for one long second, then bolted in the opposite direction, running as fast as his legs could carry him. "No, thank you. I don't need a job that badly! I'm happy being bored!" he shouted over his shoulder.

The cat watched him go, shaking his furry head.

The farther Madnes ran, more strange sights came across his path: A goose wearing clothes; a bear walking on two legs; a group of mermaids like dolphins playing off the shore…too many things that his brain couldn't make sense of.

And suddenly, Oswick was no longer boring—it was crazy.

And he might not live long enough to have a future.

❊2❊
TEA FOR TWO

"Oz, dear?"
The small child named Oz carried a tray of dough buns over to his mother. "I got them ready, Mama! What we do next?"

"Put them in the oven, slowly," she instructed. Her lips held a smile as warm as the sun. "Go on. I already preheated it."

Carefully, little Oz slid the tray into the oven. His gray eyes lit up with delight watching as the oven heat worked its magic on the dough. Soon, there would be cream-filled buns ready to eat. His most favorite treat!

"I wanna be a great baker like you, Mama," he said.

She chuckled, the sound filling him with warmth, her embrace filling him with love.

"I will always love you, Oz. No matter what happens, no matter where I am." Her eyes, shimmering like stars, took him in. "You'll remember that, won't you?"

Little Oz gazed up into her fair face.

"My love for you will never die…"

Her face faded from his vision.

Never die…

The words echoed into the distance, into the dark void…

Oz's eyelids fluttered open, waking him up to reality and leaving the distant, old memory behind.

He straightened on his perch on an oak's high limb. He hadn't come all the way here from Wonderland just to relive past memories. He rubbed his temples, waking himself up. He'd come here to observe the event that was now taking place below him.

Cheshire had called for a meeting in the world known as Earth, here on this odd island, Oswick, where both worlds touched—holding the meeting in an isolated spot in one of the humans' large parks.

The cat was going to announce something today, and that something was most likely who the next Madness Solver would be.

A smirk spread across Oz's lips. The job would naturally fall to him. He was the Red King's son. No one else was more worthy of the position!

Yes, this would be a triumphant day for Oz. He would soon have the power that came with being the Madness Solver, and with that power he would be able to find *her*…

the person most dear to him, Mother, who had vanished one day from his life without a trace.

All he needed was that power.

"Today, I come before you all to announce whom I have selected," Cheshire spoke before the gathering of Wonderlanders, which wasn't all that big, "the person who will take up the position as Wonderland's next peacekeeper, the Madness Solver. It's a big job, and one that is highly necessary. I am pleased to have the role filled once again."

Oz waited expectantly from his perch. The Wonderlanders leaned forward in anticipation.

"Without further ado, may I now present to you the chosen person..." Cheshire waved his paws for dramatic effect. "Come forth, Madnes Hatter!"

Oz almost fell out of the tree.

A boy the same age as himself, and wearing the most ridiculous top hat Oz had ever seen, was brought before the crowd. Cheshire made Madnes stand on the platform as the assembly evaluated their new Madness Solver.

Some cheered, some grumbled, and others were unsure of what to think. Through it all, the human boy sweated.

Oz quickly ducked down and hid out of sight before Madnes could see him.

Another Hatter? Oz stared, dumbfounded. "*He's* the next one? Not me?" he mouthed silently to himself. "How..." His fists clenched. "How can it not be me? And why *him*, of all people?"

That runt. That no-good son of the Hatter family.

Black feathers swirled as Oz spread his crow-like wings. He leaped off the branch and took flight in the opposite direction, leaving the park and meeting behind.

Oz stood still before the throne and tried desperately to keep a rein on his nerves. He folded his black feathered wings against his back and bowed formally. "Forgive me, Father. I have disappointed you," he spoke.

The Red King, built like a Viking from legends, leaned his thickly bearded chin on a fist, his features cold as ice. He regarded the boy bowing before his grand throne dais.

"More than disappointed," the king agreed, and Oz stilled. The red robe draped about the king's shoulders shimmered like a waterfall of blood down the giant chess pieces which made up his throne. "I spoke with Cheshire. And while I am furious with his decision, and have always hated the cat, he is the Selector. He gives the power to whom he chooses, and no one else may have a say in the matter." He shifted to steeple his fingers in a displeased manner. "In view of your potential, I was hoping that Cheshire might abandon the Hatter family and come to us. However…you apparently were not worthy enough, Oz."

"Not worthy…? But Father," Oz stammered, "I've done nothing but train. I've worked for years to be fit for the position! How can anyone call me unworthy?" The temper in Oz's voice rose, but one glance at the king and it subsided.

Father was angry—he was dangerous when he was angry. Oz shoved his own emotions aside and attempted to appease him. "Perhaps I can change Cheshire's mind. I will make him see that he has chosen wrongly."

"Hm. I hope so, for your sake," the Red King replied. Light from a partially draped window cast distorted shadows around the throne. "A useless son has no place in this kingdom."

A useless son has no place…

Oz kept the hood of his cloak up. He thought back to the dream he'd had earlier: the memory of his mother's embrace.

'Mother, what happened to you?'

The mystery of her disappearance had tormented Oz for years.

He stuffed down a cream-filled bun, seated at a pristine café just outside the palace castle.

What had happened, and was she still alive? There was only one way left to find out, after all the many ways which he'd already tried. But for that, he needed the special power of the Madness Solver to solve this dark mystery.

Nothing, and no one, would get in the way of his goal. Especially not this Madnes Hatter.

It was time for him to pay a visit.

"Did you hear the announcement?" A girl was chatting with her friend at another table. "Prince Oz wasn't chosen as Madness Solver. Can you believe it?"

"I know, right? Total shock!"

"He's handsome on the outside, but a total loser inside, I guess."

"I'm curious about that new Hatter boy, though. They say he's easy on the eyes."

Both girls giggled.

Oz furiously stuffed down two more buns.

"That was humiliating," Madnes stated as he left the meeting of Wonderlanders, his face feeling red enough to explode.

"It's just standing before the people whose livelihood and wellbeing now rests in your hands. You'll get used to it," said Cheshire cheerfully.

Madnes wanted to groan and look skyward.

"You'll do splendidly." Cheshire's paws patted his hand reassuringly. "Now, go and rest up! I'll be seeing you shortly to begin your training!"

Training. Great. He was already dreading what all that would entail.

The cat strolled off, at first on two legs then bounding away on all fours before disappearing from sight.

Madnes sighed heavily and headed home.

The next morning came, followed by school, and he kept thinking back to Cheshire's words and reliving the moment of seeing all those Wonderlander faces focused on him, watching his every movement on the stage. Some hopeful, some quietly laughing at him.

He couldn't do this. He was an introvert at heart! He couldn't...

"Your cousin is here!" called out Mom suddenly, the moment he stepped through the door, back home.

"What?!" Madnes exclaimed. But his mom just smiled down at him with that not-a-care-in-the-world expression on her face.

"I invited your cousin over for tea. He's out back in the garden. I already set the tea and buns out on the table for you," she said, and reached down to pinch his nose between her fingers. "Go on and say hi. You two used to be marvelous friends when you were little! Maybe you can rekindle that bond?"

Madnes pried her fingers off. "What for?" he grumbled.

Mom gave a carefree shrug. "You're both the same age, and he's back in town. So, why not? It would do you good to have more than two friends. Consider this a lesson in developing your social skills."

He shook his head irritably. "Maybe I don't want any social skills."

"Go on! Or does this dragon have to gnaw on your noggin?" She held up a hat in the shape of a dragon's head, its jaws open, and charged at him.

"Okay, okay!" Madnes bolted for the backyard door. "Sheesh. Why do I have to have such a weird mom?"

He stepped out into the backyard's garden area. The late afternoon light cast shadows about the trimmed bushes and overflowing flower beds and the single lattice table, which was nicely set up for two.

Tea for two, what was Mom thinking? He steeled his nerves and approached the figure already there waiting. His cousin turned his head slowly, one arm reclining across the back of a chair. Gray eyes and a face that had not smiled in years met him.

"Cousin Oz." Madnes tried to keep his voice from wobbling as he greeted him.

Oz's skin was fair where it showed around a fine suit and cravat, his layered blond hair slicked back. He resembled every inch the son of a wealthy family.

As children they had been friends, despite being two very different people from very different backgrounds. But a change had overcome Oz, like a vine of ice creeping through his soul and choking out the kinder person that he used to be, and that friendship had come to a bitter end. Whatever had caused the change was still a painful mystery to Madnes.

Sitting here, he could feel the hate pouring out of Oz even now.

Madnes awkwardly searched for something to say. "It's been a long time," was all he finally managed.

One perfect eyebrow rose—the only greeting Madnes was going to get from Oz.

Madnes sat hesitantly in the opposite floral wicker chair. Oz took a sip from one of two teacups, fine china with hand-painted yellow roses.

"Quite," Oz said. "And how has life been treating you, Madnes?" He bit off half of a cream-filled bun. Madnes watched the white cream slowly drip out. "Has anything interesting happened lately?"

The way he said it—it made the hair at the nape of Madnes's neck stand on edge.

Did he...*know* something?

❀3❀

TO BRAWL, OR NOT

TO BRAWL?

"Anything interesting? Um…well…" Madnes fidgeted under Oz's scrutiny.

Was he allowed to tell people about Wonderland? Cheshire hadn't said anything about that yet. But maybe the better question was: would anyone believe him?

"Just…busy with responsibilities. School and all that drama, you know," he ended up saying instead, and watched as another cream-filled bun vanished into Oz's mouth. "Wow, you eat a lot of those. Is that stress eating?"

Oz shot him a glare. "I do not stress eat."

"…Okay." Madnes shrugged. "How about you? Anything exciting going on? Travel plans and rich-people stuff?"

The teacup rattled in Oz's hand. How dare lowly Madnes inquire into his personal life? He could see the smug look behind those blank violet eyes of his, pretending to be ignorant and innocent. It was infuriating.

'No; I must control my emotions. I will not let such a peasant get the better of me,' thought Oz.

He would be smart about this. He would take his time and convince Cheshire that he was more worthy to be the Madness Solver, and Cheshire would then transfer the power over to him instead. He'd… But how long would he have to wait for that to happen? What if Cheshire would never consider him worthy of the power? That would make all this time and effort a waste. Could he chance that? Could he risk wasting time, here, when Mother might be alive and in danger somewhere?

"Must be nice having a wealthy family," Madnes was saying, awkwardly, trying to make some conversation. "Lavish vacations, the best education…I can't begin to imagine what that's like." He gave a small laugh. "Do they spoil you much?"

The next bun fell from Oz's hand.

"Oh, by the way, how's your mom doing? I remember your dad saying something about her having to leave the island for health reasons, years ago… What was that about?"

Something snapped inside Oz.

Madnes was still wearing a cheerful mask when a large

claw suddenly swiped across his head.

Madnes gaped, stunned, his top hat falling off. Oz's hand was the shape of a large crow's claws, five long finger-talons, and a pair of black wings stretched out from his back. More feathers made a black crown circling from behind his ears.

"Oz...?" Pain told Madnes that there were slash marks across his face. Oz leaped over the table, claws ready to slash open his chest next. But even as Madnes saw it coming, he couldn't force himself to move. Nothing made sense. The friend he had once known so well—he wasn't even human. Had he really not known anything about Oz at all?

The claws came. Madnes envisioned them ripping him open. But then, just before the claws touched, a power inside Madnes activated and made his legs move.

His whole body moved on its own—getting out of the chair and sidestepping away from Oz's attack.

Oz landed on the chair, then turned and clawed the air just as Madnes's head ducked.

Oz screamed inwardly at himself for losing his self-control and exposing his true nature. But hate had won over inside him. He would kill Madnes and steal the Madness Solver power from him by force. It was too late to switch to any other strategy now.

"W-what are you, Oz?" Madnes said, ducking and dodging the claws. "Are you something from Wonderland? Why didn't you ever tell me?"

"I've been wanting to do this." Oz sneered. "I deserve the power. Not a wretch like you who can't even use it properly."

Claws caught his shoulder and Madnes bit off a yelp in pain.

Something made Madnes fall flat to the ground and both his legs kick out into Oz's stomach, sending the rich boy staggering back into the table, upsetting the teacups.

Oz ground his teeth. The Madness Solver power was fighting back—it wouldn't allow its master to die so easily. But the Hatter boy was weak and inexperienced. Now was the best chance Oz would ever have.

Oz lunged in a dive, wings propelling him forward, both his clawed hands stretched before him and ready to tear flesh.

Madnes was still getting up off the ground. His body rolled aside from one clawed hand, but the other grazed deep through his arm as Oz flew past. "*Ahk—!*" he cried out. Madnes struggled back up on his feet, trying to block the pain from his mind. "Why, Oz? Do you hate me this much? Or is this just about the Madness Solver power?"

"I'm taking it from you, Madnes. And no amount of begging is going to stop me."

Clutching his bleeding arm, Madnes could almost see the dark hatred pouring from Oz like a dark cloud. Why was it only now that he could see it? So much bitterness directed towards him; how did he never notice it before?

"Why do you hate me? What did I ever do to you, Oz?" Angry now, Madnes's other arm lashed out to block another of Oz's swipes, while his knee came up into Oz's stomach.

Oz fell forward, but not before pulling Madnes's legs out from under him. They both hit the ground. Oz tried to get his vise-like claws around Madnes's neck. Madnes struggled to avoid the death grip.

"You're in the way," Oz said coldly. "No one comes between me and my goal. Your death is a necessity, Madnes."

"A necessity for what?" Madnes searched to find some glimmer of light, some speck of empathy inside the person Oz used to be, but the soul in Oz's gaze had long since frozen over.

Claws looped around his neck. "Don't— I can help you." Madnes could barely speak against the powerful claws closing off his throat. Nothing he could say would change Oz's mind; the person he knew was gone.

'I abandoned him to become like this, didn't I?' thought Madnes. *'I should have been there by his side. It's my fault. I deserve this…'*

Everything grew hazy, like mist slowly drowning out the world.

He couldn't breathe, couldn't swallow, couldn't think.

You have to fight!

Fight? At first, he thought Oz had spoken, but the face above him was set and grim.

Fight…if he didn't fight back, there was no hope of changing anything, no hope of making anything better, of serving some sort of purpose in this world. He couldn't afford to die, just yet.

Madnes balled up his fist and aimed for Oz's exposed throat. The punch rang with a loud *thud*, knocking the air out of Oz and sending him backwards, choking.

The claws released him, and Madnes's body mimicked the same punch-kick moves that Oz had just used on him. A powerful kick to the stomach sent Oz down into the garden's fence post.

Both of them paused for a moment, coughing and panting.

'He's using my own moves against me? The power of the Madness Solver: intelligence, quick learning, and inhuman strength,' thought Oz, as he tried to gather himself and prepare for a better attack plan.

Just then, the door to the backyard swung open.

Both he and Madnes looked over in alarm. But the person standing there wasn't who either of them expected it to be.

"Long time no see, Madnes, Oz." The gruff voice spoke around a stubble jaw.

The man entered the garden, hands in the pockets of a duster coat, his torso crisscrossed with belts and knives, and a pistol at each hip. His boots thudded the ground with every step.

"Am I interrupting somethin'?"

❀4❀

A Lost Friend

O z went wide-eyed. "Cosmic Hunter?" he exclaimed.
Madnes straightened, still clutching his injured arm.
"Uncle? Since when did you get back from the Amazon
Jungles?"

The man flashed him a grin. "I had some Tropical Killer
Cakes t' take care of, but my fork put an end to 'em. Didn't
you see me in the papers?"

"*Killer Cakes...* I'm not even going to ask." Madnes shook his head.

Uncle winked. "They may not have been cakes, exactly, but they became fine-tastin' desserts after I put an end to their rampage."

His uncle was a so-called bounty hunter — the good kind — tracking down problematic monsters and bad guys. He traveled the globe, and often brought Madnes souvenirs and grand tales of his daring escapades.

"You look hurt, there, kiddo," Cosmic observed from his stance on the patio. "Matter of fact, ya'll look in terrible shape." His rusty eyes narrowed. "Horsin' around is fine, but I think you're playing a little rough, ain't you?"

Oz took several steps back and clicked his tongue in irritation. He would have to retreat now that he was outnumbered. He silently criticized himself for acting rashly and blowing away any chance he had at winning over the power. Cheshire would never hand it over to him this way — he'd messed up, badly. And now, Madnes knew his true identity as a Wonderlander.

"Don't think you're ever safe, Madnes." Oz growled. "I'll take that power from you soon, one way or another." Oz's wings beat the air and the rest of his body transformed into a large crow, soaring past the steam of chimneys and up into the air currents.

Madnes watched him vanish into the clouds before he let himself sink down and slump on the ground.

"Let me get somethin' for that," Uncle Cosmic indicated his arm.

"You knew about all of this?" Madnes asked him, incredulous. "Wonderland and everything?"

"O' course I do." Cosmic finished patching the gash, and gave his shoulder a pat, making Madnes wince. "My baby sister was the last Madness Solver."

"Auntie Rose?" He looked up in surprise. "Then…is that why she died?"

Cosmic opened his mouth, but then seemed to change his mind, as if regretting he'd said anything at all. "Not much t' do about them cuts on your face," he said instead. "Better come up with a good excuse for 'em to your ma."

Madnes's eyebrows slanted downward. "Uncle, what happened to Auntie Rose?"

"Never you mind that, now. You've got bigger problems t' worry about." Cosmic helped him to his feet. The movement screamed pain through his muscles. "We gotta get you in better shape, boy! Just because your noggin is smart, now, don't mean your body is."

Madnes grimaced.

"That power can give you inhuman strength, and make you learn things fast, but you need an unfaltering determination in that spirit o' yours or it'll amount to nothin'."

Madnes tried to pull away from the grip Uncle had around his shoulders, wincing. "I don't know what you're saying, but I'm fine. Let me go!"

"I haven't given my fave nephew a hug in months. Don't refuse me."

"Favorite? I'm your only one!" he protested in vain.

"Your cousin, Oz." His uncle turned more serious. "Sounds like he wants t' take that power from you."

Madnes nodded reluctantly. Thinking about it made guilt well up inside him. "Who is he *really*?" he asked.

"Prince of the crowv race in Wonderland, and the Red King's son. That king rules over much of Wonderland."

"Oz is a *prince*?" Madnes breathed, stunned. "That's news to me."

But thinking about it further, it did answer some questions from the past, like where Oz's family wealth came from and why Oz had had so much trouble fitting in at school.

"He has enough power of his own. Why does he want mine?" Madnes muttered.

His uncle shrugged. "Dunno. But I'm gonna train you in some martial arts so you don't go gettin' your pretty face ruined again." He chuckled.

"Huh?" Madnes swallowed. "Do Madness Solvers often get into fights?"

Madnes preferred to keep to himself and not get involved in problems, especially fights. But this power wasn't going to allow that anymore, was it?

"Well..." Cosmic gave a vague shrug.

Madnes didn't like where this was going...

The next day, after school, found Madnes sitting glumly on a bench and staring out at the view of the sea. Behind him, in the playground, children laughed and screamed on tire swings and jungle-gyms, getting their frilly skirts and suspenders dirty. In the distance, a steam locomotive whistled its arrival, and a line of steam cars clamored through the streets. Oswick was lively today. And he wished he felt the same.

"Ohhh, Madnes is sulking again."

He didn't bother to lift his head as Alice plopped herself down onto the bench beside him. "You look like a scorched toad."

"I'm not a scorched toad."

"Oh. An angry scorched toad, then," she corrected. Madnes snorted and fiddled with the brim of his maroon top hat. "What's got you in such a glum mood swing? I hear your uncle is back; that should make you happy, right?" The green bow in her short hair had little decorative gears sewn on it, matching the gears on the side of his hat. Did she do that on purpose?

"...Yeah. But he thinks I need to toughen up. He's going to give me lessons in martial arts or something, which is why I'm not eager to head home."

She watched him, waiting for more.

"...And Oz came by," he finally admitted under her scrutinizing gaze. "We sort of...got into a fight."

Secrets couldn't be kept from Alice. She had a way of drawing things out of him, whether he wanted to talk about them or not. But maybe that's why he also found her company therapeutic. If only he could tell her about Wonderland and all the crazy things going on, too...but he held his tongue, chewing it.

"That was expected," she replied. He looked down at her with a question, and she smiled knowingly. "I heard about you and Oz from Harrey a long while back. He said that things grew sour between you two. I may not have been here when it all happened, but even I know it's a bitter thing when best friends break apart. All those emotions must have come bubbling up again when you met after so many years."

Yikes, she was perceptive.

Alice had arrived in town soon after Oz had left. And other than Harrey, she was the only thing that had helped keep

Madnes's life together.

"Things grew sour between us because of an argument," Madnes told her. He folded his fingers together, squeezing them. Guilt rattled in his stomach.

He should have been there for Oz. He shouldn't have let things end the way they did between them. He let his head fall back. "I don't know what to do, Alice. You know how much I hate admitting things, but...I really don't know what to do for Oz. He's nothing like the person I once knew, and I feel like part of it is my fault. I should've fought to keep our friendship alive. He needed me back then, but I was too much of a scaredy cat and an introvert to help him."

Alice gazed ahead beyond the sprawling sea and crying gulls. "To solve a problem, you must first know what the true problem is."

"The true problem?" He let the words mull over in his mind. "He was hurt by something I did when we were young—or rather, something I didn't do. Now, he's out to punish me and take my power away. That's all I know."

"He wants your power? He must have a reason for it."

"Yes," he said slowly, "but how can I learn what that reason is?"

Wait a minute. He'd accidentally mentioned his power to Alice, and she was acting as if it were normal...

His gaze narrowed at her. "You...do you know about me?"

❀5❀

NINJA BANANA

PROBLEM

Mrs. Snooté observed herself in the mirror, turning her stance this way and that.

"No, no, this will not do! My jewelry doesn't match."

The lady set her gold necklace on top of the dresser for a moment as she went to rummage through her closet for a more stylish blue dress.

An oblong shadow passed by the window, and something yellow flashed in the corner of her eye.

Snooté looked over her shoulder, her expression furrowed with unease.

But there was no shadow there and nothing seemed out of the ordinary…

With a shrug, she returned with another dress and reached for her necklace…only to find it gone.

"Bobby?" she shouted. "Did you take my necklace? Put it back, right now! I'll give you to the count of three!"

The child came trundling from his room to peek into the master bedroom. "What necklace?" he grumbled, yanking at the arms of a teddy bear.

"Didn't you just…?"

She fell silent and turned back to the window. It couldn't have been Bobby, not when he'd been playing in his room.

Then, realization dawned on her.

"Help! We've been robbed!!" she cried.

"You…do you know about me?" Madnes turned on the bench to face Alice intently.

Her sea-green eyes blinked back at him full of innocence. "Your family owns a successful shop in Oswick. Isn't it natural that Oz's family would want to buy the business for themselves?" she said simply. "They own so much of the town already, the greedy snobs. They rarely ever even visit Oswick."

"Uh…right." He looked away. She wasn't talking about the Madness Solver power—he was being stupid again.

Though, he wasn't sure if he should feel relieved or not. A part of him wanted her to know the truth...

Pssst!

Something tickled his ear. He craned his neck around to look, but the only things to see were the grass and a leafy tree giving them shade.

His attention returned to Alice.

Psssst!

His head whipped around again, and this time he spotted a twitching cat tail floating behind the bench.

Instinct made him want to scream, grab the nearest object and throw it at the creepy disembodied tail. But a pair of cat eyes and a floating mouth also appeared and quietly called out to him, the tail motioning for him to follow.

Great. It was that weird cat again.

With a grumble, Madnes stood. "I, um, have an errand to run. But maybe we can meet at Harrey's later?" he told Alice.

She nodded, lips holding a faint smile.

He tried to look as casual as possible while walking away: off around a bend in the park where bushes rose like a wall and hid him from sight. Then he ducked low and followed the beckoning tabby tail as it led him from the park. "What is it now, Cheshire? And just so you know, that bodiless floating tail thing is freaky."

"You will see, you will see," came the cat's voice.

The tail guided him through town, dodging bikes and steam cars, until they reached the corner of a street in the business district. "Here we are!" Cheshire announced and made his full gray body materialize, wearing a blue suit vest and bowtie. His paws gestured grandly. "Your very own Madness Solver office!"

Madnes squinted. At the street corner stood the largest, fattest mushroom he had ever seen, at least two stories tall, with windows and a door decorating its beige front.

"A...mushroom?" he exclaimed. "First of all, why do I have an office? And second of all...a *mushroom* office?"

"*Shush, shush!*" Cheshire gestured with a paw. "Its true mushroom form is only visible to those connected to Wonderland, but to everyone else it's a normal-looking shop at the corner of a busy street."

"A mushroom?"

"Get over it." The cat handed him a pair of keys. "Being the Madness Solver, you need an office where Wonderlanders can find you when they require your assistance."

"And you just had to announce it to the whole of Wonderland, didn't you? I'm still mad about how you lured me into that assembly meeting!" Madnes shuddered at the embarrassing memory: standing on stage before all those people, creatures, or whatever you wanted to call them.

"You whine too much."

Madnes's jaw fell. "I—I do not! I'm just...reclusive. Is that so wrong?"

Cheshire took the keys back and opened the glass front door, shoving Madnes through. It was a quaint office indoors and gave off the feel of a coffee shop, complete with chairs and little tables. It even had a counter and an odd-looking contraption for brewing coffee.

Cheshire inspected the dust. "You're going to have to change that introverted way of yours and become a real people-person. That's what this job requires, otherwise you will fail miserably."

"You can't expect me to become a completely different person in one day!"

"I don't. But I do expect you to try. That is, unless you'd rather spend your time learning how to make hats?"

Madnes's jaw twitched. He took off his top hat and set it on the counter. "Fine. But I can't promise I'll be perfect at—"

"Good! Your first job just came in today!" Cheshire interrupted and waved an envelope in his face. "The perfect way to begin your training!"

Still uneasy about a cat wearing clothes, Madnes asked what the job was.

"Jewelry has gone missing all across the wealthy part of town," Cheshire explained. "And no one has been able to catch a glimpse of who the thief is. They come and go as silent as a mouse, apparently." He tapped the side of his nose, "My keen whiskers tell me it could be the work of ninja bananas."

Before Madnes could roll his eyes, Cheshire nudged his chin with the tip of his tail. "You must locate their treasure horde and return the jewelry to its rightful owners."

Madnes pushed the annoying tail aside. "And how am I supposed to do that? What's the grand plan?"

Madnes held a pair of binoculars up to his eyes, observing the fancy house that sat just beyond a decorative front gate. He'd waited for what felt like hours, the sky already colored with sunset, and not a banana or ninja came in sight.

He growled at the feline beside him, "This is your grand plan? Wasting away hours staring at people's houses, and trying not to look like a creeper while doing so?"

Cheshire's paws shrugged up. "That's what a stakeout is. You'd best get used to it."

He pressed his lips into a thin line. "How do you know it's the work of ninja bananas or any Wonderlander, anyway? It could be anything—"

Something moved, and Madnes paused to shift the binoculars. A flash of yellow with an odd crescent shape passed by.

Yep, it had to be them.

Scurrying around the parked steam car they were hiding behind, Madnes drew near and pressed against the house's front gate, keeping to the shadows and scanning the area. He caught sight of movement: a yellow thing climbing out a window. It was followed by the scream of another victim now missing her jewelry.

"Ah-ha! There's the evil little banana." Binoculars up, Madnes followed as the thief made its way to the ground and sprinted across the lawn, then scrambled up and over the encircling garden wall. Madnes hurried, dashing towards the section of wall, and just caught a glimpse as the ninja banana slipped down a storm drain in the street.

"Seriously?"

Cheshire caught up to him, and they both peered down the drain. "I'll remain up here, while you go and get yourself soaking wet," said the cat.

"How noble of you," Madnes replied sarcastically and yanked the drain lid off with one powerful tug of his good arm; thankfully, the injury to his other arm was healing quickly.

Madnes hesitated for one second, then dropped feet-first down into the dark pit below.

His boots landed with a heavy splash, and he suddenly wished he had a flashlight.

"Here, you'll be needing this!" came the cat's voice.

Something fell from above and struck him on the head. Catching the object before it hit the ground, he turned on the flashlight.

"You could thank me."

"Yes, thank you, Cheshire, for nearly killing me with a flashlight," Madnes retorted.

Light on, Madnes made his way forward through the slippery, dark drainage tunnel. Beyond the ceaseless patter of dripping water, he could hear the shuffling noise of little feet. He carefully followed the sound, moving the flashlight back and forth, until finally something glinted in the light.

Madnes drew near, and there it was: a sack left open and full of sparkling gold and glistening jewelry. The sack had been carefully arranged up on a ledge of brick as if to make a large nest.

Ninja bananas swarmed over the treasure horde, yapping and hopping, and happily licking at the shiny objects. That is, until they saw Madnes.

All movement ceased. Beady banana eyes stared up at him from beneath ninja headbands. And then…they attacked.

Hundreds of little feet and sharp fists came at him, pointy heads jabbing and poking at his previous injuries, while fists beat at his face searching to pound out his eyes.

"*Eeyaaag!* You rotten bananas!" he screamed.

"Madnes? What's happening down there?" Cheshire craned his neck down at the drain.

SPLRSH! Madnes sprang out of the drain head-first, his body swarming with ninja bananas like stinging bees, and Cheshire tumbled over backwards.

"Do something!" Madnes shouted, waving and shaking his limbs—doing anything he could to get the evil yellow creatures off. Cheshire swiftly snatched the sack of jewelry from his fist.

"You'll have to appease them," he said.

"Appease them *how?*" Madnes shrilled. He kept yanking the yellow things off and they kept jumping right back on, jabbing at him and kicking with their ninja feet, their high voices screaming at him in some gurgled language.

"By finding them a new shiny object they can keep," Cheshire explained with infuriating calmness. "They love shiny things and horde them in the same way that many bird species do."

"Shiny?" Madnes moved his head painfully, looking this way and that. "What else is there that's shiny?"

His boot crunched on something. He shoved bananas aside to look down at the object and found a shard of glass.

His eyes lit up with an idea.

Madnes limped and ran, ninja bananas clinging to him for all they were worth. Several people on the streets stared his way as he hobbled and groaned—they couldn't see the bananas, only a teenager waddling and limping for no apparent reason.

He tried to ignore the humiliation of it all until he reached the glass factory's garbage disposal bins. "There, look! Look, you rotten bananas!" He pointed. "Lots of shiny stuff. And you can have all of it!"

There before them, heaps of stained glass shards glistened in the sunset's light in a myriad of colors, all shiny and not unlike jewels.

"Oooogh," the bananas awed as one, staring at the mass of shininess before them.

One by one they slipped off him and waddled over to the colorful bins. He sighed in relief and rubbed at the countless bruises now discoloring his body.

"First mission well done!" Furry paws clapped together and Cheshire cast him a whiskered grin. "Now, to return the jewels to their bereft owners…"

Madnes shot him a weary scowl.

❀6❀

Under Suspicion

"Madnes, be careful!"

"*Ssshh!* I am being careful." Madnes glowered over his shoulder at the cat and then continued forward stealthily.

One step at a time, he approached the glass doors, the fading sunset reflecting off their surface. He neared at a low crouch, just close enough for his arm to reach, and set the satchel filled with missing jewelry down on the doorstep of the local police station, nudging the satchel forward with his knuckles. Not a soul was on the sidewalk but him, at the moment.

Cheshire motioned with a frantic paw for him to hurry back.

Madnes kept his head low and trotted back to the alley. "I don't like leaving all that jewelry there. How soon will the police find it?"

Cheshire's shoulders shrugged. "We don't have an option. There's no better way to get the jewels back to their numerous owners than this. And we can't risk you being seen or they'll pin the crime on *you*."

Madnes waved a hand. "Yeah, yeah, I know." He peeked around the alley corner, watching the lonely satchel. Why was no one coming out of the station? Were they off getting their coffee and pastries? He chewed nervously on his thumb nail.

A shadow rolled across the pavement. Madnes started and looked to the source: a man dressed in rags and a worn down hat was approaching the satchel.

"Is he going to…he wouldn't, would he?" Madnes tensed. "Just great! I knew I shouldn't have listened to you." He stood, and Cheshire tugged frantically at his maroon jacket.

"Don't go—you can't risk being caught!"

"But…" He looked back at the beggar. The man's grimy hands lifted the satchel.

Darn, he had to stop this!

Madnes sprinted out of hiding, ignoring Cheshire's yowl.

The beggar saw him and stumbled back in surprise. Madnes grabbed for the satchel. The man growled and turned so that his grab missed it, and then the beggar broke into a run, fleeing the police station.

"No!" Madnes regained his balance and chased after him down the sidewalk.

'I have to get it back!' he screamed inside his head. Power suddenly surged in his legs, muscles burning as if a fire had been lit inside them, and he found his body running faster. He caught up with the beggar and jumped him from behind, crashing them both to the ground.

It was a struggle, but he managed to grab hold of the satchel and with a heavy yank pull it free of the man's rope-tight grip.

Madnes stood, a bit wobbly, and the beggar turned with a snarl before scuttling away.

"Ha! That's right. Don't mess with Madnes Hatter!" he told the fleeing figure. He dusted his hat off from the ground where it had fallen and put it back on his head.

"Is that so?" spoke a deep voice behind him.

Madnes whirled around. The last bits of evening light showed a tall, looming man behind him.

"Who are you?" Madnes asked cautiously.

A baby-blue left eye regarded him from beneath thick black eyebrows. A black eyepatch obscured the right eye—decorated with a little silver rose and a pair of white wings. The man could have been considered a handsome twenty-something—with his lean form, layered black hair, and clean-shaven jaw—except for the suspicious frown that seemed permanently etched into his façade. Madnes took note of the badge decorating the left breast of his uniform.

"I..." the man began and his thick eyebrows drew near, making Madnes lean back away, then the guy snapped upright and spun on his heel like some Tai Chi master; the spin stopped and he posed dramatically, "...am Inspector Jacque Coolette. *Cool*—ette. And bringing down crime is what I do best!" Flicking a hand, he then posed like a hot-shot for a poster.

Madnes drew back with a frown. "Another weird person..." he muttered.

The inspector gawked at the remark and nearly fell over. "You dare to insult me?"

"Here." Madnes shoved the satchel of jewelry into his hands. "It's your problem now. Bye!"

Coolette blinked down at the mass of jewelry for a moment, then exclaimed and hurried after Madnes, "Thief! You dare defy the law?"

The man's footsteps pounded the pavement after him. Madnes thought he could outrun the guy, but the inspector was fast and not far behind, legs moving like an Olympic runner.

"I didn't steal anything! If I took it, would I be giving it back?"

"None can comprehend the twisted mind of a criminal. You are under arrest!"

Madnes quickened his pace. The running steps behind him slowed, and for a second he thought he'd lost the guy. But then something slashed through the air, not far to his right.

He glanced back and saw Coolette tossing a length of rope, aimed at Madnes's legs to trip him—the rope taken from a giant spool statue in front of a knitter's shop.

"You just stole that rope!" Madnes yelled, trying to distract the fierce inspector.

"Borrowed!"

"What's the difference? I could say the same thing!"

The rope flew forward and tangled in Madnes's legs. He stumbled, and the inspector caught him by the elbow. The guy's angry and suspicious face blocked out Madnes's vision.

Coolette raised the satchel, his single blue eye glaring at him and demanding an answer. "Are you telling me that you *borrowed* this?"

"Someone else did! The bag was in front of the station, and that beggar tried to take it. I stopped him, and I gave it back to you."

Dark eyebrows lowered suspiciously.

"You don't have proof that I did anything wrong," Madnes reasoned, swallowing down his nerves. "If anything, you saw me rescue it from that beggar."

Coolette rubbed his sleek chin in thought, leaning uncomfortably close.

Madnes stood his ground, sweatdrops beading his forehead, and waited until the guy finally straightened and nodded. "There is truth behind those words." The blue eye glinted. "But do not think I don't still suspect you of something sneaky, Hatter boy. I've got my *eye* on you." He turned so that his one good eye faced him pointedly.

Madnes leaned far back, giving him his own distasteful expression. "Goodbye, then, and good evening," Madnes said and forced himself to keep calm, turn, and march away. He could feel the man's stare following him.

"I'll be watching you, Hatter. Always watching you..." Inspector Coolette posed in what he must have thought was a cool, intimidating posture. Then his foot caught on the "borrowed" rope and he stumbled.

"That guy's a bit dense in the head, isn't he?" Madnes said, once he was far enough away. Only Cheshire's eyes and cat mouth hovered visible above his shoulder.

"And a bit of a klutz, too. Good thing for you." The feel of a paw smacked the back of Madnes's head. "I told you to be more careful!" the cat chided.

Madnes huffed and bit the inside of his cheek.

❋7❋

POWER FOR A PRICE

After having evaded Inspector Coolette's grasp, Madnes made his way through the downtown maze of twists and turns until the *March's Repairs* workshop and garage came into view. It was an uneven, two-story structure with mix-matched roofs and a clock tower jutting through the upper portion of the workshop. Giant wheels, spindles, clock hands and a cluster of different dials made the upper half of the building resemble a living clock.

Madnes raised a fist to knock, when the metal door of the workshop suddenly swung open.

A mop of fluffy brown hair and stray blue highlights appeared out from a cloud of dust: Harrey. He pushed back his green visor glasses, blinking. "Madnes! It's about time, you slow poke!" He grinned, grabbed Madnes by the arm, and pulled him inside.

Madnes waved away the dust. Alice was already there at one of the less cluttered counters in the shop. An assortment of gadgets and equipment in need of fixing lined every wall and shelf of the place. They navigated around metal bookcase aisles, over to the counter, its surface covered in old stains.

Harrey's uncle had been running the workshop since he could remember — a family business that had been there since the beginning of the town's founding. Harrey worked with his uncle and lived up on the second floor.

Madnes noted that Cheshire had disappeared. He frowned; that cat had a way of appearing and vanishing whenever he felt like it.

He took a metal stool on Alice's right. She was fiddling with a swirly straw made to look like an elephant trunk, and she gave him a secret smile. There was only one reason why Harrey invited them over — it was always the same thing.

"Wow, dude. Are those *bruises* all over you?" Harrey pointed out the combat wounds from ninja bananas peeking out from his sleeves and collar.

Yeah, there was no way he could begin to explain those.

"Just the kind of day I've been having," Madnes mumbled quickly. "So, what did your new invention damage this time?" He smirked at the pouty look Harrey then gave.

"It didn't damage anything! Why do you always assume that?"

"Because that's what always happens."

"You don't even know what I invented, yet!"

"By all means, do show us."

Harrey instantly brightened, and Madnes found himself being dragged through the workshop and into the adjacent garage. The ceiling soared high overhead, the walls stretched out just as wide, offering a generous amount of room in which to build and test machinery. Alice trotted behind them, a smile around the lollipop she plopped in her mouth.

Harrey dug through a mess of junk metal and objects before finding what he was looking for—dragging it out with an excited *Whoop!* He stood the contraption on a space of clear floor before them.

Madnes's frown twisted to the side and one eyebrow rose. "A bicycle?" he asked.

"One that can *fly!*" added Harrey with glee.

A big propeller sprouted up from the bike like an umbrella, and a smaller one stuck out from the back seat. Harrey hopped onto the seat, feet on the pedals, and began pedaling. Both propellers started to turn, slowly at first, then gaining momentum.

The blades whizzed and hummed, growing so loud they had to cover their ears. Gradually, and a bit wobbly, the bike rose a foot off the ground.

"See, *see?*" Harrey exclaimed excitedly. He pedaled faster, and the bike gained more height.

Madnes watched and crossed his arms, while Alice cheered their friend on.

Something crackled.

Madnes shook his head and shut his eyes, not bothering to watch what he knew would happen next.

Sparks crackled from the blades and the bike came crashing down, Harrey yelping along with it.

CRSH!

Pieces of debris scattered across the floor, and a screw rolled to Madnes's boot.

"Wow. It lasted a whole five seconds. That's a new record for you."

"Oh come on, Madnes," Harrey whined, pulling himself painfully from the wreckage and hobbling. "Don't squash my dreams, dude."

Madnes shrugged, palms up. "You do that just fine all on your own."

Harrey's tanned face pouted, eyes moist. Madnes exhaled and glanced away.

Ever dramatic Harrey was like a slice of the sun that couldn't stop beaming when he was happy, and a miserable deluge when he got depressed.

Alice stepped between them. "That's not true. Harrey, you come up with splendid ideas! Even if they...don't always work."

"That's an understatement," Madnes muttered. "*Ouch!*" A brown heel jabbed him in the shin, and Alice's look shot him a warning.

Madnes turned his face away, making a pout of his own. He knew he shouldn't be so moody and shouldn't be taking out his frustration on his friends, but he'd always had a hard time controlling his emotions.

Later, seated at the only clear counter space, Harrey asked what they all wanted for a late dinner.

"Toast and eggs for me. I like night brunch," said Alice.

"Pizza." Madnes let his tired forehead bump the countertop, his hands limp at his sides. All his bruises still throbbed.

"Looks like you might get a scar there."

"Huh?" Madnes lifted his head back up, and Harrey tapped the side of his face where three claw marks were still healing—made by Oz.

"Oh. Yeah, maybe," he said. "I can look even uglier than I already do. Yay."

Alice laughed into her palm. "Madnes, you've never been ugly. Some girls at school even think you're cute."

"Really?" He stared at her, unbelieving. "Maybe they should have their vision checked."

Harrey laughed and slapped the counter. "I doubt anybody could beat you in a contest for best dry humor."

Madnes chuckled at that.

A cuckoo clock interrupted them, the mechanical bird springing in and out of the carved wood clock, announcing the late hour. As if on cue, a small robotic creature came walking from the kitchen with a large tray held high. It hopped onto the table counter and delivered a platter of toast, eggs, and pizza slices.

Madnes squinted at the small robot, or to be more precise: the frog robot. Its bronze body gleamed beneath a small tux and bowtie as it walked upright on long, thin hindlegs.

"A waiter frog. You couldn't just build something normal, could you?" Madnes commented.

"You fixed him!" Alice reached and patted the glossy metal. "It's been a long while since I last saw him."

Harrey grinned. "He got run over by a steam car. Took some time to fix him up. But he's his old helpful self again, aren't ya, Frobbit?"

"YES. I AM FUNCTIONING NORMALY-ribbit." Round glass eyes flashed yellow as the robot responded.

"See? I can make something that works." Harrey stuck out his tongue.

Madnes dipped his head in acknowledgement.

"ARE YOU DISPLEASED WITH YOUR PIZZA?" The frog turned to him. Madnes blinked down at the small robot. It moved forward, gears clanking and creaking, and suddenly took the plate and threw the pizza in his face.

"Yuck! Why'd you do that?" Madnes peeled cheese and sauce off his nose, then swiped a hand at the robot.

The frog leaped, easily dodging him.

"YOU DID NOT EAT YOUR PIZZA. YOU ARE A BAD BOY-ribbit." It grabbed the toast and eggs and began throwing food at each of them.

Alice ducked under the counter.

"Make it stop!" Madnes shouted, trying to snatch the hopping frog.

"Coming!" Harrey called, as he grabbed a flyswatter with one hand and shielded his face from fire with the other. He aimed a swat at the frog's back, pressing the shut-off button.

"BAD BOooy…" The frog's battery died, and the glow left its eyes.

Staring down at the mess of dripping eggs and pizza sauce everywhere, Madnes headed off to find the bathroom and cleaning rags. "Yeah. You really made something that works."

Harrey carried the frog over to a shelf of gizmos awaiting to be fixed. "It *will* work! Eventually."

After cleaning up, Madnes remembered with a start that he'd forgotten to call home and let Mom know where he was. He now picked up the garage phone's teal receiver, dialed in the number, and left a message for her saying he would be at Harrey's a while longer.

Thank goodness she wasn't there to pick-up and scold him.

As he left the message, he fiddled with the buttoned cuff of his maroon sleeve. Some pizza stain lingered on it, but at least the color wasn't much different from the jacket.

He spotted something dark peeking up from under the sleeve: something like ink marks.

Madnes dropped the receiver and pulled his sleeve back to discover an image inked in black on the inside of his wrist — the image of a numberless clock, both hands at where the 12 o'clock should be. He stared intently at it, a mix of feelings washing through him. As he watched, the long inky hand moved one tick from the 12 o'clock mark, and the gap in between flooded solid black.

"What *is* this?" He rubbed at the mark, scratched it with his thumb.

The clock image wouldn't smear.

He tried water, scrubbing at it, but the ink remained unaffected.

"How did…?"

His arm quivered. The air about him grew heavy, and his breath quickened. *'Don't panic, don't panic,'* he tried to tell himself. But a horrible gut feeling was writhing inside him.

This clock was counting down time.

His time.

Madnes hurried past the sink, past the counters and clutter. Harrey and Alice looked up in surprise. But he didn't stop until he stumbled out of the workshop and the cool night air hit him. The air felt humid from a mass of gathering clouds overhead.

"Cheshire! You must be around here, somewhere. Come out. Now! Tell me what this is?" he called out to the dark empty street outside *March's Repairs*. He waved his wrist up in the air.

Only silence met him, and a single dog barked in the distance.

"What..." he let his arm lower, eyeing the clock on his wrist through shaky vision, "...is this?"

An uncontrollable tremor rattled his body. He'd never felt so shaken in all his life.

"Am I..." His dry throat tried to swallow.

"...Dying?"

⚙8⚙

Rules Like Chains

Cheshire watched from behind a cluster of hawthorn bushes, while Madnes's shout rang through the still night. His furry ears drooped.

"This is the one thing I hate about this job…" he whispered to himself, furry gray forehead wrinkled.

"But it is the necessary price that must be paid."

Time passed Madnes as if he were in a fog—as if someone else were moving his legs and waving goodbye to Harrey and Alice as they parted ways to head home. He vaguely heard Mom scolding him and trudged up the staircase, into his room, plopping onto the bed.

He curled up, trying not to look at the inked clock beneath his sleeve. Trying to shut his eyes, even though his racing pulse wouldn't let him sleep. Trying not to think, even though his mind was running through a grim valley filled with images of death.

When the pale break of dawn finally came, it was small relief. He shoved all the grim worries inside a locked closet in his mind and got himself back into a normal state of being for school—or as normal as he could manage.

His pulse didn't slow, but at least he made it through classes that day. He had to hold on until he found Cheshire—then he could let his emotions erupt. He had a bone to pick with that snazzy-dressed cat.

It wasn't until the afternoon, when he wandered out to the Madness Solver mushroom office, that he at last laid eyes on the gray tabby.

Madnes marched over, shoved back his maroon jacket and white shirt sleeve, and held up the inked clock image, his height towering over the cat. "Explain," he demanded of Cheshire.

Looking uneasy, Cheshire's paws motioned for him to cool down. "Yes, I was going to get to that part—once it showed up."

"And no sooner? It's *my* life on the line. I have a right to know what's happening!" He held the clock above the cat's brow. "Auntie Rose died young, and she was the previous Madness Solver." He had to pause to swallow, even though his throat was dry. "Is the same thing going to happen to me?" he asked.

Cheshire met his gaze for what felt like a long somber minute before he answered, carefully. "The Madness Solver power puts great strain on the body. And it...has certain rules."

Madnes's eyebrows lowered under a mountain of questions. But the first question he asked was, "Is there a time limit on my life?"

"The power thrives by feeding off the life of its host. Depending on how strong the life force of the host is, determines how long it will take before it's all consumed. And it also depends on how frequently you draw large amounts of power to use. It all factors into how fast or slow the clock ticks," the tabby explained, and he pretended to clear dust from his brown hat.

"And when the long hand reaches the 12 mark after going all the way around again?" Madnes asked and tried to hide the tremble in his voice.

When Cheshire hesitated to answer, he shook his head knowingly.

"It's ticking down my life. This thing I wanted nothing to do with is slowly killing me. And I never had a say in it, did I?"

Cheshire's frown deepened. "The Madness Solver must always exist...for the sake of Oswick and everyone in it. It is a price that must be paid."

"And it must be paid with my life?" he exclaimed, rage trembling his fists.

"I won't pretend you should be glad of this—nor not resent me for it—but you *must* accept it. Or else, you won't be able to move on and fulfill your duty to this island and to Wonderland."

"Why *me*?" he whispered through clenched teeth.

"The power has rules which even we in Wonderland do not understand," Cheshire explained, hopping onto a table stool, and standing like a teacher, hat in one paw and gesturing with the other. He raised one claw.

"One: life force is the price paid for wielding the power.

Two: you cannot tell anyone about it draining your life. If someone figures it out, you must keep them silent.

Three: the host must be mostly human.

Four: the one chosen must have the right spirit for the job. A determined will that cannot be shaken, and a caring heart."

He placed the hat back on his furry head. "Those are the qualifications for becoming the Madness Solver. And those qualities tend to run in your Hatter family."

Madnes faced Cheshire squarely. "And you really believe I'm any of those things? Well, besides human, I mean."

"You *will* be. If you shape yourself up and stop dwelling on self-pity."

"Self-pity?" Madnes gawked. "Excuse me for being unhappy that some crazy cat came along and changed the world I live in and cut my lifespan in half."

Madnes stormed out the glass office door and down the town's sunbaked street, not waiting to hear anything more from Cheshire.

The sea splashed merrily against a pebble beach, and a group of kids played in the waves, squealing with delight.

Above the town and its wisps of chimney steam, an airship hummed slowly on its way past, followed by seagulls riding the air currents brought in from a faraway storm.

Madnes watched the scene.

How long did he have? How long would it be until he could never see these tranquil shores again?

The thought struck Madnes that he would miss this. Boring as things were in Oswick, and as much as he had wanted to get away, the thought of leaving this life forever hurt.

He would miss the dusty crimson sunsets that colored the waves purple; the children in the playground who always found something to giggle about; the fireworks during Christmas; Mom's silly laugh and her homemade soups; the lantern festival, folding and gluing together paper lanterns with Alice and Harrey, and the frilly dress that Alice would probably wear; Harrey's grin as he showed off his next flawed invention; Madnes getting his driver license and one day his very own steam car; graduating, and having to figure out what he was going to do with the rest of his life; and Oz…fixing their severed bond.

Every cherry blossom spring, every heatstroke summer, every colorful and hot chocolate autumn, and every snowy winter wrapped in hand-knitted scarves from loved ones…how much longer before it would all be taken away from him?

"I thought…" His fingers dug into his crossed arms as he gazed towards a future he once took for granted. "I thought I would have forever…"

He chuckled, a dry sound that lacked any mirth, and his vision watered over.

"What a spoiled brat I've been."

It was too blurry to see the sea anymore, nor for a soul to see where he should go from here.

The inked clock on his arm burned through the tears.

"I feel...lost."

❀9❀

THE ROAD AHEAD

"Well now, that's an honest confession, if I ever did hear one."

Madnes shifted to eye the person who had interrupted his private moment: a rough, rugged man leaning on the railing causally beside him, duster coat rustled by the sea breeze.

"Uncle Cosmic. How did you know where to find me?" Madnes tried to wipe away any traces of tears with a sleeve.

Uncle shrugged his broad shoulders like it was obvious.

"I ain't a world-renowned bounty hunter for nothin', boy. Besides, you were supposed t' meet up with me and begin your trainin'."

Madnes grumbled and looked away. What was the point of training, now? For what? It meant nothing if he was going to die by this blasted power anyway. He could have a few years or only months left to live, and then what would be the point?

"You don't have t' hide your fears behind a mask, Madnes." Rough fingers clasped his shoulder and deep brown eyes held his gaze. "I know what's goin' on—same as what my sister went through. Though I didn't find out about the power sappin' away her life until it was too late…"

Madness swallowed so his voice wouldn't tremble. "You know about that? Don't let the cat find out—apparently there are rules that say nobody's allowed to know."

Cosmic chuckled at that.

"So, there's no way out of this?" Madnes asked.

Cosmic thinned his lips and gave a single headshake. "Far as I know, no Madness Solver's ever been able to outlive the power's ticking clock. But hey, that don't mean there's no way t' be found—"

Madnes threw up his hands, the urge to scream welling in his throat. "They died because they didn't have enough time to find a solution—if one *even* exists! My chances are the same as theirs. How can I expect to end up any differently? Just…leave me alone to wallow in my misery." He made as if to go, but the hand on his shoulder anchored him to the spot. He shot a glare at the bounty hunter.

"You don't want t' die, and that's gatherin' turmoil inside ya. I won't blame you for that, lad. It ain't somethin' you asked for," he said with his gruff voice. "But life don't just end when we die, Madnes."

"How would you know?" Madnes said bitterly, and chewed his cheek, using the pain to keep the tears in his eyes from spilling over. He pushed against the hand anchoring him.

"Tell me." His uncle leaned back, elbows on the rail, though the grip of his hand did not ease. "When you put loads of effort into writin' those short fictional stories of yours—creatin' characters after your own heart—don't you care about 'em?"

Madnes gave a little nod, unsure where the man was going with this. How did he know about his secret writing hobby, anyway? Mom must've found out and spread gossip.

"A painter cares about his paintings, a sculptor his sculpting, a musician his music, and a writer his stories," said Cosmic. "A creator cares about his work. So then, how much more do ya think our Creator cares about us—especially us being living, breathin' creatures and not some stiff painting or words on a page?"

Madnes's gaze wavered uncertainly.

"That's why life don't end when we die, lad. That's why the Creator calls us back to His home, like a guardian calls his child. No matter what happens here in this life, we can be reunited there in His home in the end, if we believe in His *Word*. So, quit moppin' about life." He gave him a lopsided grin. "You're still breathin' right now. Use what you've got and get things done! You were chosen for a reason, and it's time you figured out why. Maybe you'll be the Madness Solver t' change everything, eh?" He clapped him on the back.

Madnes wasn't sure if he fully understood Cosmic's words, or if he believed the Creator actually cared about him, but something about it made his mind stop sinking into the quicksand of despair he'd been feeling trapped in.

"C'mon, let me take ya out for some Italiano spaghetti."

"Spaghetti?" Madnes blinked. "Food? At a time like this?"

The guy's muscled hand slapped him on the back again, knocking the air out of his lungs. "Yer a growin' lad! And it'll make you feel better. Food soothes the soul as well as the stomach—every man who's a man knows that!"

"...If you say so."

"Two orders of yer finest *spaghetti carbonara and meatball-surprise*, ma'm!" Cosmic ordered, before Madnes had a chance to peer at the menu—not that he would've ordered anything, anyway. He wasn't in the mood for eating. Especially pasta. And something about "meatball surprise" felt unnerving.

The Italian restaurant was a quaint place with red-tile flooring and fish-catcher nets with lanterns for hanging lights. Their round, metal dining table had clock gears decorating the sides, and Madnes frowned at the reminder of time passing him by. But once the dishes arrived—spaghetti covered in cheese, sauce, veggies, and oddly shaped meatballs—the aroma did, for a moment, distract his mind.

Cosmic dug into the pasta the moment it touched the table. Madnes watched, then sighed and poked at the spaghetti with his fork before taking a bite. Yep, it was delicious. So was the meatball and its strange egg yolk surprise.

"See? Food's good for a mopin' soul!"

"I wasn't moping," he grumbled at a fork of cheesy mushrooms. He twisted the fork around and around, gathering noodles in a spiral. "I don't know how long I have, but I don't want it to be wasted away. I promised myself I would help Oz. Even if I fail at this Madness Solver job, keeping my promise to him is the one thing I can't fail at—no matter what."

A toothy grin creased Uncle's face.

"What?"

Cosmic shook his head of rugged curls. "Nothin'. *Heheh.* Good to see you've got a goal t' live for, now. It's a wonder what a meal of fine Italian food can do for you."

"It wasn't the food," Madnes protested. He sat back and exhaled. Truth was, the change of scenery and a reminder that he wasn't alone—that there was more beyond this life—was washing away the gloom.

"All I know is I have to keep myself alive for everyone else's sake. Question is, though, how?" he pondered.

Cosmic finished slurping up noodles and dabbed a napkin at his lips. "'Tis a mystery, kiddo! Uncharted waters, as they say. But," he held up a finger, "one thing is sure: Avoid using that power. And when you do have to use it, use it wisely."

"I don't want to use it, *ever*," said Madnes. "But it's like the power forces me to. I can *feel* it—like a part of my body, a hand or something—and I can't help but use it. Just like I can't help using my brain to fix problems."

"Hmm...not much choice, then." Cosmic pondered, thumb rubbing his stubble jaw. "But if we can build up your body and mind, n' make ya more capable, maybe the power won't feel like it has t' always do stuff for you. That might buy ya some time—maybe enough t' find a real solution."

A weight of worry lifted from Madnes—a small weight, but once it left, he could feel the difference. And the world seemed a shade brighter.

❄10❄
Let's Go to the
Drop!

"Last day of school, *last day of school*!" Harrey jumped up and down like an excited rabbit high on carrot juice. He wrapped an arm around Madnes and Alice each as they headed out the front doors for the last time that semester.

"We passed our exams, our finals, and I managed not to get a D in Algebra. We gotta celebrate!"

Alice tried to keep her growing grin at his enthusiasm subdued. Her eyelids, however, felt as heavy as lead after all that studying.

Madnes looked ready to drop and sleep on the street at any moment. Maybe a little celebrating would wake them all up from the many study all-nighters they'd pulled off.

"What do you suggest we do, Harrey?" she asked.

He pondered and blew back stray bangs from his eyes. "*Aha*, I know just the thing! Let's go to The Drop."

A part of Alice suddenly regretted asking him.

Madnes went wide-eyed. "The Drop, are you out of your mind? Only insane folk go there!"

"I'm pretty sure I'm still in my own mind." Harrey felt about his scalp as if checking. Madnes rolled his eyes to the sky. "C'mon, Mady, I've been wanting to take you guys there for so long. It's beautiful! Not to mention a paradise for thrill seekers!"

Madnes raised a hand to halt him. "That's the thing: it's for thrill seekers. I'm not a thrill seeker. I'm a happy-to-be-on-the-ground-in-my-tucked-away-cave seeker. And don't ever call me Mady."

"*Boooo*, that's no fun at all." Harrey made a face. "I'm gonna change that attitude of yours, Madnesy. We're going to The Drop and having ourselves the experience of a lifetime!"

Alice had to muffle her laugh at the return expression Madnes gave. He was neither outgoing nor a risk taker, and The Drop required both. She poked his shoulder playfully. "Afraid of heights, are you?"

Madnes mock rubbed where she poked him. "Anything that's dangerous should be feared; that's just normal instinct.

Nutjobs like Harrey are missing those instinct gears in their brains."

She giggled. Despite his words, Madnes seemed in a better mood lately, for some unknown reason.

She sighed inwardly. He was handsome in a simple sort of way, if you could see past his cynical, introverted remarks. His eyes were a gentle violet, his lips were perfect arches, and he had a funny habit of chewing his thumb nail. She looked over; he was doing it right now.

She knew him well enough to know there was more than what showed on the surface. At heart, Madnes was loyal and caring. But he was also realistic, and to him much of the world was a cynical and dark place.

"Let's give it a go, Madnes," she prompted him with a smile. "For Harrey's sake. You might even enjoy it!"

He stared at her in horror.

Madnes watched the airship gliding overhead, its massive torpedo-shaped balloon and spinning propellers appearing now closer than ever before. The ground elevation here brought the sky uncomfortably close. But it was easier looking up than it was looking down, and so he kept trying to keep his gaze up.

His feet carried him nervously up the wood planking of a winding staircase, up the side of a steep cliff face. The waterfall's rush of thousands of tons of water spilling over the cliff and into the depths filled his ears like a giant's constant rumble. The air felt thick with moisture forming misty clouds of droplets.

Harrey was enjoying himself immensely, head turning every which way as they climbed, and Alice looked awed.

So, Madnes swallowed and let his gaze drift down to observe his surroundings.

They were nearing the top of the massive waterfall and its steep cliff face that curved like a giant horseshoe. It dropped the height of several cliffs before cascading deep into the earth down a hole-shaped cavern, where no light could reach. Beyond the waterfall cliff spread a scenic view of rock pinnacles and cliff balconies, and where a chasm ripped open the ground, the waterfall's submerged river flowed freely out into the open. The river wound its course through the greenery, creating islets, to meet with the sea in the far distance.

The horseshoe-cliff walls rose to either side of Madnes, and everywhere along them adventurers were hiking. Some were even crazy enough to hang by a piece of V-shaped fabric and glide down the scenic cliff and massive canyon to the bits of grassy islands below.

"I refuse to do that," he said instantly.

"But it'll be *fun!*" Harrey pulled him by the arm up the last few steps, and they stood on top of the horseshoe cliff. The river rushed past them with hurricane force.

Madnes's body trembled like a leaf inside that hurricane. "Your definition of fun and mine are VERY different."

Harrey waved over one of the Glider Lodge staff, ready and waiting to outfit customers for a scenic flight down the cliff and following the river out. He handed over cash before Madnes could protest.

Madnes felt Alice's reassuring hand pat his back. "The Drop just looks scary. But we'll be attached to the safety line. See that rope?" she pointed. It ran from the Glider building and down at an angle like a rollercoaster, slanting through the air toward the low river before leveling out.

"Jumping off a cliff and hoping you can fly your way

down...where's the sense in that?" he muttered.

Alice shook her sun-blonde head.

Before Madnes could urge his feet to run in the opposite direction, he found himself buckled to one of those absurd, death-defying V-shape contraptions called a glider, and both his hands were gripping the steering bar before him.

Harrey went first, his glider attached at the top to the safety zip-line, and launched himself off the cliff edge at a run. Madnes's lungs flew into his throat in fright, just watching. "*Wahoooo!*" echoed his friend's wild laugh.

Alice turned and gave him a wink before she faced the cliff and charged forward, just as Harrey had done. Madnes panicked when the ground left her feet. But she giggled, gliding away like a graceful heron.

Madnes's limbs shuddered, making his glider's fabric shake.

"You're next," motioned the staff member.

He didn't want to. Every inch of him screamed against it. But the worry that something might happen to Harrey or Alice while he was here being a lame scaredy cat made him more sick to his stomach.

"Oh the heck with it!" he shouted to the air, and he forced his feet into a run, eyes shut until the last moment. The ground suddenly bid his shoes farewell, and there was nothing but open air and a steep drop beyond his comprehension. The rush stole the scream from his throat, and his mouth hung wide open and silent, eyeballs bulging.

Behind him, the waterfall dropped as he did, and when he turned his face, he could see rainbows scattering the heavy mist rising in clouds. It was beautiful.

Directly below, the cavern hole swallowed the waterfall like a giant gulping mouth. The zip-line angled him down towards it, and Madnes gripped the bar for dear life.

Just as it seemed they might all crash one by one into the monstrous dark pit, the zip-line suddenly rose and leveled out, and they sailed past. Dipping at an angle again, the line carried them through the horseshoe canyon, following the rushing river as it carved its way through the terrain. It was like another world, trees perched on soaring rock pinnacles and cliff terraces. He was terrified and shaking and unexpectedly exhilarated.

It was petrifying. And it was beautiful.

Facing the fear, the unknown depths, and discovering that he was able to fly...it felt like a metaphor for what he was facing with the Madness Solver power. And now, he was actually enjoying the view, despite his hands being frozen stiff to the bar like a dead man's.

Plok!

Hm? What was that sound?

Rip-p-p-pk!

Black things like arrows ripped through the glider's supporting fabric.

Madnes's breath hitched.

The glider descended like a falling bird.

❀11❀

SKY FALL

The fabric ripped and popped as a volley of black arrow-like things pelted the glider. It felt like a surreal dream—the glider losing air through the tears, causing it to lose altitude and descend.

Madnes tried not to panic while lifting his gaze to see the rips above his head. Surely, the safety zip-line would stop him from plummeting to his death?

Then he felt a jarring tremor followed by a loud *Snap!*

The sudden strain had either been too much, or another black arrow had cut the rope. He heard and felt both the clamp and rope that connected his glider to the safety zip-line snap.

There was a momentary pause while he hovered serenely in the air, and then the glider stalled and descended towards the canyon below. His frantic heart leaped up his throat, smothering his scream.

Vaguely he heard something. Alice or Harrey, was it? But both were far ahead and had no way to turn around and help him. What help could they possibly give, anyway? Funny, he'd come along on this trip to make sure they didn't get hurt, but now *he* was the one falling to his death.

It wasn't being the Madness Solver that would kill him, after all. No, just a glider accident.

Heh, it was almost humorous.

Those black arrows, he thought, where were they coming from? One zipped by, its sides lined with black feathers.

Must be from a very large crow. Interesting the random things you notice when you're about to die.

He looked out to where his friends should still be flying. There was Harrey at the front. And behind him another glider was...falling? He couldn't tell at first because it fell at the same speed as his. There were rips and holes in the other glider's fabric, and it was lilting crazily.

'Alice!' his mind shouted.

Whatever had damaged his glider had done the same to hers. He couldn't accept Alice dying with him. She had a long life ahead of her. And he still wanted to keep however much of his own he had left!

The power—he had to use it.

Madnes let down the wall inside his mind which kept the power at bay, and a surge of knowledge and strength came flooding through into him.

You've finally let me through, now that you need me, hm? An airy voice spoke inside his head, and the translucent image of a young female with fairy wings glowed behind his eyelids. *I suppose I don't have much choice but to help you. If you die, I'll have to hop over to someone new—and I'd really rather not, just yet.*

A light flashed, and his mind and body suddenly began to work without him while he watched.

He tried to ignore the canyon walls around him and the river chasm growing below, as his hands moved on their own—removing his jacket and spreading it against the glider's thin framework, covering up most of the rips and holes. The updraft rising from beneath him held the jacket in place, and he fished out safety pins from a pocket his mother had stuffed (*who knew why*). His fingers worked quickly, securing the jacket to the intact portions of fabric. The jacket now acted as a temporary patch, but it wouldn't last for long if he couldn't level out the glider. Wind flapped and pushed against the patch work. But there was something he had to do first.

No. It's too risky to save her. I refuse.

"What?" Madnes shouted at the strange fairy-person inside his head. Somehow she must be linked to the power, or was she the power itself? "I'm saving her—with or without you. You may as well help me so we can all survive!"

Tch. Stubborn humans… But it is one of the things about you that fascinates me, heehee.

Madnes gripped the steering bar and angled it towards Alice's glider.

The wind roared past his ears, and he didn't dare glance down at how defined the river and foliage below were becoming.

His mind raced for ideas until he caught up with Alice. Coming from behind and above, he undid the straps that were holding his legs up and let them dangle down. He then reached both his feet through two of the holes in the fabric of Alice's glider wings and, once through, bent his knees and locked his feet together—basically turning himself into a makeshift clamp; Alice's glider was now attached to his.

The strain burned his leg muscles, but he refused to crumple and instead drew more power.

His legs steadied, and her glider stopped lilting beneath him. He used his own glider to steer them both and try and level out.

A hawk soared the air not far to the right. Madnes shifted the gliders, steering them toward the bird. There he found what he needed: a strong updraft, which the hawk was using, and it filled out the gliders' wings and crude patchwork.

The sudden fill of air slowed their descent, and at last, they were gliding—or falling with style. And to anyone watching from the cliffs and ledges around the canyon, it must have looked like a crazy, daring circus performance.

Alice couldn't see him. The only thing she could see, and knew, was that she'd been falling uncontrollably until a pair of legs came through the glider wings above her head. She recognized the shoes, and she wondered if this was all some terrible dream.

It was a long ride down to the ground, and they had to steer clear of pinnacles and clawing branches. Beyond the horseshoe canyon were patches of clear land, where the cliffs became rolling landscape and stretched onwards toward the sea, the river below racing to kiss its salty counterpart.

Madnes pushed the bar, and the gliders curved down before making a rough landing. He released his leg-hold on Alice's glider so it could land first.

He flew ahead a ways before crashing his glider to the ground.

Bruised and battered held a whole new meaning for him, these past few days.

Alice hopped out, and he hobbled over to her. "Are you okay? No—clearly you're not, but—"

Alice hugged him tightly, buried her head in his chest, cutting off his sentence. Not knowing what to do, and suddenly feeling awkward and a rising blush coming on, he turned his head up to the sky.

A black winged figure circled in the distance. He couldn't make it out well, but he could feel eyes on him before it veered and soared away.

'No, it couldn't be… Was that Oz?'

The black feathers. He glanced down at a piece of feather still stuck in the fabric.

He wanted to get rid of Madnes—that he expected—but Alice, too?

Madnes couldn't forgive that; he wouldn't forgive that! Their quarrel had nothing to do with Alice or anybody else. This was between him and Oz, and he would make him answer for this if it *was* his doing!

His hand moved to touch the fading claw mark scabs on the side of his face.

Harrey finally made his way through the long grass over to them. He grabbed them by the shoulders, asking over and over if they were really okay.

"I'm fine. Really. Nothing that a few days can't heal up, anyway," said Madnes.

"Good. Because I gotta ask you something."

"What?"

"Is your hat super-glued to you? Because how in the stars is it still on your head?"

Madnes adjusted his maroon top hat, the goggles and decorative gears still in place. "It's a hatmaker's secret that I won't divulge." He turned to the wrecked glider. "Are we done here? I've had enough near-death excitement for one day," Madnes said and tried to gather up his torn jacket.

"Yeahhh, just one more thing."

"What now?"

"How did you do it?"

"Do…what?" He blinked at Harrey, wrapping the jacket up nervously into a ball.

"You held up another glider with your crossed legs! Are you kidding me? Anybody else would've lost their legs trying to pull off that stunt! You must be super strong. And you managed such a neat landing, too."

"*Erm*, well, I wouldn't say it was neat…"

"But still!" Harrey leaned close. "That isn't normal, dude. That's a miracle!"

Madnes fumbled for words. And then the recoil hit him.

He fell to his knees and grasped his wrist. It felt like part of him was being sucked out, his body's life force ripping from his being and going into the wrist—no, into the clock inked into his skin.

He raised the wrist up to see: The long hand had moved four ticks, and the black ink filling the space of his used-up time widened to fill the gap.

Madnes swallowed and shut his eyes.

"What is that?" came Harrey's voice beside him. "Say, what's going on?"

"*You cannot tell anyone about the power draining your life—that's one of the rules,*" he recalled Cheshire's words.

But could he tell them about the power in general?

Should he?

That would mean having to explain Wonderland, too, and the strange situation he'd been caught in. Would it put them in danger to know, or would his friends be better off not knowing?

'Alice almost died, even though she knows nothing of Wonderland—it didn't matter.'

His friends were in danger now, whether they knew his secrets or not. So…he may as well spill the beans, right?

Oz almost chuckled, watching from afar in the azure sky. "I'm surprised he survived that… The power truly is incredible." His gray eyes narrowed. "I've rattled his little world, though, and that was certainly worthwhile."

Madnes wouldn't rest easy knowing that even his friends were no longer safe—that his Madness Solver job was putting them all at risk, as well as himself.

Friends…hm. Oz wondered how short of a time it had taken for Madnes to forget all about him—back when they were kids—and move on to his new friends…

"Ah, Madnes. You will soon be broken and beg me to take your cruel power away from you. That will be your punishment; I will watch you unravel and beg for your existence to be no more than a bad dream. And then," his hand clenched, "with the Madness Solver power transferred over to me, I will find *her*."

❀12❀

QUEST FOR THE

GOOSE

Madnes wanted to tell them about Wonderland. About the strange creatures he saw. About this crazy power he was forced to live with until his numbered days came to a swift end.

What came out of his mouth instead was:

"It's...well, it's this place that...that..."

Madnes had no words to describe it—any of it. How do you explain something so bizarre that people would be convinced you belonged in an insane asylum?

"...It's this new job I have," he fumbled. That part was true. "The work makes me strong, I guess, and...the clock is a symbol-thing for the job."

There. All true, just vague.

"Huh?" Harrey and Alice both tilted their heads to the side, bewildered.

Madnes fidgeted under their blank stares, then he straightened himself and began the long walk back to The Drop without another word. He didn't wait for them to follow; his cheeks were red enough as it was.

Why couldn't he just tell them? *'Because it sounds too freakishly crazy, that's why!'*

He would have to mentally prepare them first, or give them some sort of proof beforehand. Yes, he would tell them—eventually. When he didn't look like a buffoon that'd gotten hit over the head with a glider too many times.

The next morning, Madnes opened the glass door to the giant mushroom-of-a-building he was forced to call the Madness Solver Office.

"Did something happen yesterday?"

Madnes stumbled in surprise and caught himself. There was Cheshire, bright and early, and looking dapper as ever.

"Nope. Nothing of importance to you," he murmured in reply, hanging his top hat on a hook.

He was wearing his spare maroon jacket, the other being repaired from the glider ordeal.

The cat adjusted his blue bowtie and eyed him sidelong. "I'm not quite sure how I'm supposed to take that..."

"With fish and chips, if you like."

"Haha. Clearly the power has been improving your sense of humor."

Madnes went over to the coffee maker—an odd contraption fueled by steam as it heated and bubbled water before blasting it into the coffee grounds.

He got a full pot boiling. He would need it. Now that school was out for the summer, and Uncle Cosmic kept waking him up at ridiculously early hours to train, the last thing he wanted to do was be stuck inside a musty office lacking air coolers on a muggy day.

He wasn't sure which was worse: the stuffy scent of the office, or the scorched pavement of the town as it baked under the sun.

"Are there ice cubes? I'd like to turn this into iced coffee."

"In the basement."

Cheshire followed him down, paws folded behind his back like a watchful mentor. "So, you have a better understanding of what's to be expected of you now, yes? How the job works?"

Madnes pulled out a bag of ice from a large ice box. "To be honest, I don't get the point." He headed back upstairs to the brewing coffee. "Just what all is in this Madness Solver job description? Do you have some sort of check list or something I can follow?" He couldn't help saying it with added sarcasm.

"As a matter of fact, yes." Cheshire pulled out a rolled paper tucked inside his blue silk vest. "Just printed it this morning."

With a stupefied look on his face, Madnes took the sheet and read:

"The Purpose and Duty of the Madness Solver"

❖ *To keep the peoples of both worlds in harmony.*

❖ *To keep those who know about Wonderland quiet: not allowing them to spread word to the rest of Earth nor start a possible battle of the worlds and other such drama.*

❖ *To act as mediator between worlds, and the representative of Earth to the Wonderland Kingdom.*

❖ *And to help keep watch with the current Cheshire over all portals connecting both worlds.*

Madnes finished reading and looked up at the cat, who now stood on the countertop to be eye-level with him—a mentor should be taller than his pupil, after all.

"You do realize I have no idea how to go about doing any of these things, right?" he stated plainly.

Cheshire nodded.

"Keep the peoples of both worlds in harmony?" he read again. "How am I supposed to do that? I can't make the people around me listen to anything I have to say, let alone people I don't even know!"

"There are Earthians who would love to get their hands on Wonderland, and likewise there are Wonderlanders who would love to get their hands on Earth. There are predators and masterminds on both sides, and it's your job to make sure they behave. It's quite vital. But don't get your knickers in a twist just yet, Madnes. You will learn, and you have the power to back you up—that power is quite important in making people listen to you."

"Predators *and* masterminds?" He folded the paper and put it in his jacket pocket with a newfound anxiety. "Speaking of the power—" he began.

Suddenly a bell jingled, cutting him off, as the front glass door swung open.

Something short entered the office, and Madnes had to lean over the counter to see who or what it was.

The most pristine woman approached them both, wearing red-frame glasses and a matching red handbag, complete with a fancy bonnet on her graceful head. Only, she had a beak for a nose, and a long white neck. In fact, despite her pristine attire and snooty aura, she was a goose. A rather large goose, compared to regular gooses in Oswick; she reached well above his waist. Her wingtip feathers like fingers adjusted the glasses perched above her beak as she eyed the human and debonair cat.

"This is the Madness Solver Office, if I am not mistaken?" Her voice matched her pristine looks, and a flowery perfume hung in the air.

"Indeed it is, Madam Mother Goose!" Cheshire swiped his hat off and gave a bow.

"Mother…Goose?" Madnes wanted to exclaim but a sharp cat-boot heel met his big toe, silencing him.

"What can we do for you, madam?" offered Cheshire.

"It's my precious yet so naughty son, Ugly," she replied, resting her handbag on the counter. "He's gone and disappeared. I need you to find him and bring him back to me. But safely, mind you—not a feather on his head may be harmed!" A handkerchief that she suddenly held dabbed at her bird eyes—much larger and more eyelashed than normal Earth birds.

"What is his full name?"

"Ugly Duckling Goose."

"Where was he last seen?"

"Last night, at our home in the Shoe. I tucked him in bed."

"Hmm." Cheshire looked to be taking notes. "Any ideas as to where he might have gone? Does he have a favorite hiding place or a secret getaway?"

"None that I know of." She frowned as bitterly as her bill would allow. "Are you done questioning me? This valuable time should be spent searching for him, not lollygagging around with questions!" She blew into her handkerchief. "Ohhhh, my poor Ugly. Poor, poor naughty Ugly!"

Madnes bit his cheek. Lollygagging? What a demanding, snooty fowl... He wanted to snatch that handkerchief away.

"Yes, well, I think we have enough to start on, then," said Cheshire, taking care to ignore Madnes's incredulous expression. "We'll get on the case, straight away, madam. We'll find your Ugly, don't you worry about a thing!"

"Oh." The handkerchief vanished and the tears stopped; the goose returned to her pristine self now that she'd gotten what she wanted. "Good, very good. I expect to hear from you soon." She walked—waddled—to the door. "Remember: not a feather harmed!" she emphasized, as if she were the queen herself.

"Of course." Cheshire bowed again, and the bell jingled her exit.

"Mother Goose from the nursery rhyme? And a snooty one, at that?" Madnes was finally free to exclaim.

"A descendant. What, are you surprised? Where did you think all those stories came from? For hundreds of years Madness Solvers and select people have known about Wonderland and traveled its world. Then, some got the horrid idea to turn what they saw into folk tales, and then into books. Like that Lewis man: turning our world into a story for profit. How rude is that? Making money off us is what it felt like." Cheshire dusted his paws, irate. "People in those tales were based off of real people, only twisted into a stranger version." He nodded to Madnes, "Like the Hatter family, and the March's—"

"Wait, hold up! My ancestor was that crazy lunatic? I refuse to be compared to him."

"Not as crazy as they made him out to be in the tale. Just a bit like your mother is, I'd say."

Madnes was about to protest, then thought better of it. Mom *was* a bit quirky.

"And are you the original Cheshire?" Madnes leaned forward, studying the feline through narrowed eyes.

"Goodness, no! I don't have a mad giggle. And I don't float about in pieces! *Erm*, well, maybe sometimes—when it's necessary. But I absolutely never mad giggle! It was my fool of an ancestor who they got that Cheshire impression from." He sniffed.

"Family history. Who ever would have guessed?" Madnes finally sipped his finished iced coffee. "Maybe I should write a book, too, and make some money…"

A paw pinched his ear. "Do, and I'll haunt you for life."

"You already are." He fended off the paw. "Why is Mother Goose here, anyway? And you—any of you Wonderlanders—why do any of you want to live here?"

He had always wanted to leave this island and go exploring, yet here these creatures were leaving their magical world to come to this boring place? It made no sense.

"Madnes, it's rude to pry," Cheshire said. But at his sidelong glare, the cat relented and shrugged his furry shoulders. "Why do humans want to live on the moon?" he asked him instead. "It's airless, waterless, freezing, and you could never enjoy taking a shower again. Yet, people still want to try it out. Well, it's the same thing."

"...Huh?" Madnes squinted.

"Hoping for a better life in a new world—that's what it is, Madnes. That feel of getting a fresh start, and the excitement of exploring someplace new. We aren't that much different from you Earthians, in that respect." He showed a toothy cat grin.

"*Now* you look like your crazy ancestor."

The grin wiped off. "I'm not as fluffy." Cheshire tore a paper from a little notepad he'd jotted notes on and placed it on the counter. "We should get going to—"

"Cheshire."

"Hm?" The cat was busy looking away, clearly still offended.

"Has the power ever...spoken to you?"

At that, he turned, wide cat eyes locking on him. "Spoken? Is that what you said?"

"...Yeah."

Cheshire's reaction made him wonder whether he should have mentioned it or not.

"There are a few strange rumors passed down from previous Cheshires about the power, but nothing more. Are you certain it actually spoke to you? Did it have an appearance?"

"Ah, well, it sort of had wings like a fairy: those glistening, see-through kind. And there was a lot of white everywhere and mist. I'm not sure, it was hard to tell. But...it was definitely a person of some sort." Madnes let his voice drop. An uneasiness took hold of him. "Do you know what it could be?"

Cheshire's paw rubbed his furry chin. "An old power from Wonderland, something ancient and forgotten? I'm not sure, Madnes. But it may be worth looking into during our spare time."

"You've got plenty of it right now." Madnes's arms crossed.

"Don't be silly. I have to help you find Ugly. You're still a rookie at this."

"*Pssht!* How hard can finding one gosling be? Besides, I need to start somewhere on my own without clinging to a cat's tail for guidance—pardon the expression."

Cheshire raised a furry eyebrow, studying him, then placed his miniature hat back on his head. "Very well, Madnes. Show me what you're capable of. And, in the meantime, I'll hop over to Wonderland's library archives and see what I can dig up."

❀13❀

STALKING MADNES

Something was going on with that Hatter. Something he wasn't even willing to tell his best friends about. And it made Harrey pout and grimace just thinking about it. "Says he has some *new job,* huh? What new job?"

Harrey's gaze fixed blankly ahead, not paying attention to anything but his swirling thoughts. Hands in pockets, he didn't watch where he was going on the sidewalk until he bumped into something that yelped.

A short blonde stepped back from colliding with his chest, rubbing her achy nose. "Harrey, get your head out of the clouds and pay attention when you're walking!"

"Whoops. Sorry, Alice."

She grabbed his arm suddenly, startling him, and pulled him off the sidewalk and behind a garbage bin. "W-wha?" he stammered. She released him and he fell backwards on his backside. "Whoa, Alice. Look, I know I'm attractive and all, but you and me just wouldn't work out."

Her hand clamped over his mouth, shutting him up. She wasn't looking at Harrey. Instead, she peered stealthily from around the bin, her focus on the opposite side of the street. He tried to crane his neck sideways and see, pushing against her hand.

"Mam-mif?" he tried to say through the hand. It was Madnes she was watching, unmistakable with his carrot-red hair and maroon top hat. "Fwat he fwooing?"

Irritated, Alice finally released her hold over his mouth, and he spluttered, "What's he doing? And more weirdly, why are you stalking him?"

"I'm not stalking!"

He gave her a knowing look. "Admit it, girly. You've got the hots for him."

"No, I do not!" Her face reddened. "That's not why I'm— Just shut it and listen, Harrey! Madnes hasn't been himself lately, and I want to find out why. I want to see this *new job* of his."

"Ohhh." The lights finally dawned in Harrey's brain. "Okay. But you still got the hots for him."

"Shut it!"

He dodged her slap. "You didn't deny it."

"Be quiet! I'm on a mission here. Either butt out or keep up. I don't have time for this!"

Madnes was on the move, and Alice dashed out from behind the concealment of the bin, sprinting several yards before ducking behind the shadow of a street bench.

Harrey clumsily followed, bumping into things and tripping over his feet. She rolled her eyes.

Finally scooting up close beside her, Harrey peeked from around the bench arm for a better look at their quarry.

Madnes waved away a puff of steam from a passing steam car as he headed towards the edge of town: to where the Shoe—Mother Goose's home—was supposed to be.

A nervous chill ran down his back suddenly, as if pairs of eyes were watching him from somewhere.

Madnes quickly turned around, scanning both sides of the street. There was nothing there but a few pedestrians minding their own business.

"Hmm…" He exhaled and rubbed the goosebumps from his arms.

"You idiot!" Alice's fist came down over Harrey's head. "You almost gave us away!"

Harrey rubbed at a rising lump on his noggin. "Okay, okay! I tied my shoelaces. See? I won't trip again." He pleaded for mercy. "I gotta admit though," he peeked out at Madnes's fading back, "he sure is up to something…"

How do you go about finding a lost duckling—*erm*, gosling, or whatever it was?

Check the nearest pool or waterway? Fountains?

Well, whatever the answer, he would start at the Shoe house. It seemed logical to begin at the missing person's dwelling.

"Beware..."

The word rasped in Madnes's ear. Jitters crawled up his spine and he turned around sharply, expecting some horrid Wonderland monster. Instead, what hovered before him like a butterfly, was a thing he could only describe as a rocking-horse with dragonfly wings.

"Of what?" he asked it.

"Beware..." it rasped again. "Oswick sinks further into danger. The Red King wills to take all for himself. Beware the portals!" The insect rocked back-and-forth and wheezed, like a prophet in trance. "Seven crystals—you must destroy them all! *Destroy them aaall!*"

The horse head shook and whinnied. Wings buzzing, the insect rocked up and away, off into the clouds as he watched.

Madnes stood there.

"Okay. Yep. Wonderland is weird. I should be used to this by now." He sucked in a breath. "Moving on!"

Harrey and Alice had both watched as Madnes gazed up at the air and spoke to nothing.

They both shared a look.

"Is he okay in the head?" Harrey wondered.

The buildings and bustling faded as Madnes reached the edge of town. Here the houses and odd lopsided structures were spaced farther apart, mingling with fisheries and farmed patches of fields and distant forests.

He scanned over every bit of water he came across, but no Ugly was there.

A large silhouette in the shape of a shoe came into view.

Why a goose family would want to live in a giant shoe, he had no idea. He crossed the grass field leading up to it, tall stalks clawing at his pants. It looked like your classic weathered, brown leather boot, complete with undone laces, only magnified to house-size and with windows poking out.

"Living inside a shoe in the summer on a hot day…yeah, not something on my bucket list."

He knocked on a leathery thing like a door. But after waiting, no one answered.

He pressed his face against a window but saw no one home.

Hmm, what to do now?

'Hey, fairy-power thing in my head. Could you give me a hint? Don't use up my life force or anything, though! Just give me a little hint. You're super smart, aren't you?'

No answer came—his mind as silent as a still pond except for his own thoughts.

He grumbled. It had been worth a shot.

"Okay. So, I gotta figure this out on my own."

He stepped back and forced the wheels of his brain to turn. "If I were a gosling with a bossy, prissy mother like that, where would I run? Far away…never to be found…"

He thought and thought.

"Oh no." An idea suddenly hit him. "It'd better not be *there*. Surely not. No, he wouldn't dare to go there…would he?"

"What is Madnes *doing*?" Harrey peeked from behind one side of a tree trunk, while Alice peeked out from the other.

In his vision, he saw a ratty abandoned shack out in the middle of a field, and Madnes there wandering around it.

"Is he planning to break in? Has he finally hit his wits end and turned to the dark side? And now he goes around vandalizing abandoned shacks when no one's looking? Oh, lost brother of mine! What has befallen thee that your heart hast now grown tainted with evil's darkness!"

Thunk!

"Youch! Alwice, you mwade me bwite my twongue~" Harrey moaned.

Madnes startled and turned around at the sound, looking their way.

Alice quickly yanked Harrey down to the ground. "*Rats*, he heard that."

"Who's there?" Madnes called out tentatively.

She shoved Harrey's face down into the dirt to silence him and pressed herself as close to the ground as her body would allow, hoping the grass would be enough to hide them.

Madnes's footsteps approached.

❁14❁

WHERE IS UGLY DUCKLING?

Half an Hour Earlier

A gray gosling sniffled. Tears dripped down his beak as he slowly waddled aimlessly at the edge of a corn field.

"Hello, little goose."

Black feather wings like a crow spread wide, revealing a young man with slick-back blond hair and frost cold eyes.

Ugly hopped backwards, startled, and craned his neck to better see the boy's face.

"I'm sensing that you are upset," spoke the crowv boy. "Is it your mother? Is she being mean to you?"

Ugly wiped gray pinions across his damp beady eyes. He wasn't sure who this crowv person was, but he looked genuinely concerned and even offered him a consoling smile. And Ugly needed someone to vent to right now.

"She never plays with me…she's never there… And when she comes home after work, she just bosses me about and gets angry when I make a mistake." He sniffled. "And I hate living in that old shoe!"

The crowv shook his head understandingly. "What a wonderful coincidence this is for you, then, meeting me here today! I happen to know of a lovely place—a sacred pond, in fact—for birds of the water, such as you. Why, you could make a nice home for yourself there, away from your bossy mother."

"A home? All my own?" Ugly asked.

The crowv nodded.

"Where is it? Oh please, do tell me!"

"Of course." A dark smirk curled one corner of Oz's lips. "I'll gladly help you."

The Present

Alice held her breath as Madnes's footsteps drew near to their hiding spot.

Harrey's mouth was stuck in the dirt but his eyes roved back and forth like a rabbit about to be caught.

The footsteps paused, and for a long second there was silence…

Then the footsteps drew away. Madnes must be leaving. Alice let out a breath in relief.

"What are you doing?"

"*Eep!*" Both she and Harrey jumped to their feet at Madnes's voice, and he stepped from around the tree trunk, arms crossed, eyeing them suspiciously.

"Oh, Madnes! Hi! We're just...um...not doing much. That is..." Alice stammered.

Harrey stepped aside and pointed an accusing finger at her. "She's stalking you."

Alice's fist to his ribs staggered him sideways.

Madnes looked from one to the other. "Yeah. Sorry, Harrey, but Alice isn't like that. Which means, this must be your doing."

Harrey's jaw dropped. "You wound me, brother! Why am I always the one who gets blamed for things? This was *her* idea!"

Alice tried to hide her reddening cheeks, turning her face away.

Madnes simply shook his head. "I thought I felt eyes following me. Now, come to find out, it was just my stalker friends. Thanks a lot."

Harrey gave an awkward laugh. "Can you blame us? We know you're up to something. You're not your usual self, we've both agreed. The question is," he leaned forward suspiciously, "what trouble is it you've gotten yourself into?"

Madnes clamped his mouth shut and backed up. "I told you: it's my new job."

"What kind of job?" Harrey crossed his arms and eyed him sideways with one eye. Alice stood beside him, also waiting.

Madnes looked from her to him. "It's...it's like a..." He thought quickly while they waited. "Like a town assistant."

"A *what*?"

"You know, assisting the town, doing odd jobs, keeping things in check." He gestured with his hands, like it was obvious.

Harrey squinted. "A bouncer?"

"No!" Madnes let out an exasperated sigh. He didn't have time for this; he needed to find Ugly Duckling before the day ended. There was an uneasy pit in his stomach that Ugly might be in trouble. Plus, Cheshire wasn't here to help.

"Look, I don't have much time to explain. The town has this special duck—*erm*, goose. It's gray and very important, and I have to find it. It got loose, and I've searched every pond and water source on this side of town and found nothing."

"You're looking for a town goose?" Harrey tilted his head. "Huh, I didn't even know our town had one. That's awesome! I mean, it makes no sense whatsoever, but it's awesome!"

Madnes resisted the urge to roll his eyes. Alice was staring at him; he met her gaze and she looked away.

"So." Harrey's face puckered into his deep-thinking mode. "This is the case of the missing goose, eh?"

"You're not Sherlock Holmes. Don't even try that look."

"If I were a goose, and ran away from my fancy town pen, I wouldn't want to just go and live *anywhere*. No no no," Harrey emphasized and shook a finger. "I'm obviously a snooty goose, and I would want to go live in an equally snooty place. The best of the best of ponds!"

Madnes's stomach churned. "That's what I was afraid of," he admitted. "There's only one place like that I can think of, too."

Harrey and Alice flanked him to either side, looking off in the direction as he spoke the name of the place.

"The Sacred Pond."

Madnes dashed into a run, the tread of his boots scraping the pavement, his friends coming not far behind. If Ugly *was* going to the Sacred Pond, he could end up dead. Nothing living was allowed inside that pond. Any creature or bird who ventured into its waters was shot on sight.

But Ugly wouldn't know that; he was young and wouldn't know the rules of Oswick.

"Madness Solver!" someone shouted at him. Madnes almost lost his balance, head turning this way and that to see who'd shouted. "You still haven't found my naughty Ugly?"

There was Mother Goose. She pecked at his backside angrily, and he leaped away several steps, turning to face her.

"I'm getting him *now*! Don't worry, madam—everything will be fine soon! Do keep your beak to yourself, please." He hopped back into a run, and her beak frowned and hissed angrily after him.

Harrey shared a look with Alice as they jogged past the goose who, to them, looked like nothing but a tossed paper bag moving in the wind.

"Madam? Does he have invisible friends, or did he believe that bag was alive?" whispered Harrey. "He's spiraling, Alice, I tell you. It's all downhill from here."

"Shut up and run, rabbit-brain." Alice quickened her pace to reach the Hatter boy and his tilted top hat that somehow stayed on. "Madnes, if the goose *is* there, how will we get in to rescue him?"

"Yeah, cuz everything that nears its bank gets blasted into smithereens, duh!" added Harrey.

"There's a live camera feed—part of a recent tourism attraction, outside the pond's compound," Madnes explained between pants, jogging uphill. "We can have a look at it and see if Ugly is in there or somewhere nearby. If he is, I'll hop the wall and get him out before he gets shot...somehow."

Madnes kept his sight fixed ahead, wondering how he could pull something like that off if worse came to worst.

And what if he was already too late?

"Why is the pond sacred?" Alice asked near his shoulder.

"It stems from an old story. One of Oswick's myths," he replied. "Long ago, a boy was dying from an illness. He saw the pond, and with his last strength he crawled until he reached the water, hoping in vain that somehow the water might heal him. It didn't, of course, but he caught the attention of a being who rose from the water's surface. Some say it was like a fairy or a great nymph. The being felt sorry for the boy and allowed her power to touch him—healing him instantly. He survived and spread the tale, and ever since then the pond became a sacred symbol of ancient power. But if you ask me, it's more an attraction for tourists than anything else."

"A nymph...do you think it's true?" asked Alice.

Madnes gave an unsure headshake. What with all of Wonderland's strangeness, he wasn't sure if he could cast aside every Oswick myth as being false, anymore.

"I'm gonna go get my flying bike!" Harrey shouted at their backs.

"What?" Madnes frowned over his shoulder. "That thing doesn't even work!"

"Does now. I fixed it! And we'll be needing a get-away vehicle to pull off this stunt, right?" Harrey grinned eagerly and adjusted the work goggles perched on his head.

"We can't wait for you!"

Harrey flapped his hand at them. "Don't need you to. I'll catch up with you guys in a flash!"

Madnes groaned as Harrey sprinted away. "I hope we won't regret this…"

⚙15⚙

THE SACRED POND

Thick stone walls rose around an oval plot of land—a pond of the purest blue water at its center, glistening like a liquefied jewel. The Sacred Pond.

Madnes and Alice finally reached the pond's compound, both of them out of breath. Guards stood at every gate, and tourists flocked about with their gizmo cameras.

Madnes spotted a line of people waiting to get into the surveillance room: to get a peek inside the Sacred Pond via its live camera feed. They got in line, and he shifted from foot to foot. Time was wasting; why did there have to be a line today, of all days? If Ugly was already inside...

Something flew past in the sky.

Madnes's whipped his head around. Ugly? Did he just fly over the walls?

"There's no time for this!" he told Alice.

Madnes did the only thing that he knew would work, and which would embarrass his introvert self. He hollered at the top of his lungs and started moving people aside, shouting: "Fire! There's a fire in the building! Run!!"

He hated fibbing. But a life was on the line, and there might be real fire soon enough anyway.

The crowd waiting in line stirred into a panic and dispersed, running this way and that to see if it was true. Madnes seized the opportunity and barged his way inside the surveillance room, Alice on his heels. They looked to the many monitors hung about the cozy tourist space.

Something moved past one of the screens: a gray bird landing in a tree beside the pond.

"It's not a goose," Alice observed beside him. They watched as, within seconds of landing, red lasers flashed crossed the screen and the bird was vaporized.

They stood there, slack jawed.

"They really will kill anything..."

"I see a goose!" Alice suddenly exclaimed, and he jumped in his boots.

"Ugly? Where?" He tried not to panic, searching the screens.

But wait, Ugly was a Wonderlander. So how could Alice see him?

Yet there he was: a gray goose in flight, steadily approaching the high walls of the oval compound.

"Ugly! Turn back, you birdbrain!" he wanted to shout through the screen. Instead, they both scrambled to get back outdoors and head for the walls.

"Every door is securely locked and guarded," said Alice. "How are we going to get in and save him?"

"I told you." Madnes veered left and screeched to a halt before a section of the high wall. He backed up. "It's this new job. I can do things, now—unusual things." He focused, and inside his mind he called out to the power. *'Fairy, lend me power—just a touch...'*

Before Alice could ask what sort of things he meant, he crouched and sprinted into a run at the wall.

He heard her exclaim. Just before hitting the wall, though, Madnes jumped and the tread of his boots caught and scraped against the stone as he ran up the wall's side—the power's momentum and strength carrying him up the vertical surface.

Inspector Coolette was minding his own business, enjoying his day off work, and visiting the Sacred Pond compound.

He liked to make sure that things were in proper order— that's what days off work were good for! A chance to see that everybody was behaving and doing their job to perfection, and that no criminal was lurking about unpunished.

He had just taken his lunch bag over to a bench, where he could eat while observing the compound's walls, when someone sprinted past him at an abnormal speed. And that same person, unbelievably, scaled up the wall—not with hands but with running feet!

Coolette pulled out his weapon: the chomper, to halt and apprehend the daring criminal. "Stop in the name of the law!" he shouted, and then fired.

Pa-chomp!
Something struck the wall inches from Madnes's right side: a metal skull with snapping jaws open wide, connected to the end of a coiled metal spring.

The chomping jaws drew back, coiling away from the wall face, then sprung at him a second time. *Pa-chomp!*

Madnes lurched away, but in so doing lost his foothold and balance. He plummeted.

The skull chomper recoiled back to its owner, the metal spring condensing until it became a staff with a skull head in the hands of an eyepatched officer.

Madnes pulled himself off his sore backside where he landed on the pavement.

A pair of wings on the man's eyepatch fluttered—Oh, Madnes had seen those before. "Inspector Coolette." The man who thought himself to be the coolest thing since cucumber sandwiches; if only he had brains to match the all-knowing persona that he tried to emit.

The inspector's one eye went wide in recognition, then narrowed to a slit. "Hatter boy."

Just then, the flapping and whistle of wings passed by overhead.

It was Ugly!

"Sorry, no time to chitchat!" Madnes turned back to the wall, running up it once more.

The inspector raged, and the skull weapon chomped after him again.

"Law-breaker! You dare breach the Sacred Pond? You are under arrest!"

Pa-chomp-chomp!

"Stop, this instant!" His thick eyebrows writhed as Madnes dodged each strike and reached the wall top. "Idiot boy, you'll get yourself killed!"

Alice watched helplessly from the ground. Madnes spared one look down at her, just in case it was to be his last, and then he jumped.

Timing his momentum, and with both hands raised, he came up underneath the gray gosling as Ugly descended into the pond compound.

Fingers caught goose legs, and Madnes pulled Ugly Duckling to himself.

Together they fell to the trees surrounding the Sacred Pond.

Madnes used his body as a shield, preparing himself to be vaporized.

⚙16⚙

TRAPPED

Honestly, human, do I have to do everything for you? spoke the fairy inside his head, her purple gossamer wings flicking. *If I didn't know better, I'd say you were annoyingly suicidal.*

Madnes's eyes popped open, and before he could think of a reply, his body moved on its own—rolling off the tangle of branches he'd landed in and tumbling down to a ground thick with vegetation that made up the Sacred Pond's encircled space.

Burning lasers struck the tree within a breath after him.

Thick ferns cushioned his fall, and he laid there on his back, steadily breathing, holding Ugly tightly to his chest. Thankfully, the young bird had sense enough to keep quiet. Maybe seeing the death lasers had startled him. Or maybe it was the strange lump of ashes on the ground nearby, remnants of a laser's work and some poor creature's remains.

Fern leaves swayed across his vision and he tried to gather his bearings. They were inside the forbidden compound now, and if they were detected, the lasers would find them. They had to keep low.

K-chnk, k-chnk.

"S-something's in here looking for us," Ugly murmured, his feathers trembling against him.

"Yes…" It did sound that way. "Keep your head down."

Madnes set Ugly beside him and twisted his body around so that he lay on his stomach and could peer between the ferns. The noise was clunky and metallic, and with horror he realized it came from more than one source.

He crawled around carefully, searching for a better view. The pond's surface shimmered pure azure a dozen feet from where they'd landed.

Loud cranking and spinning gear noises came from robotic sentries. They were positioned in a circle around the compound's enclosure, and having detected an intruder lurking inside, they were now moving as one, like a net closing in.

Gears and spokes stuck out like clockwork machines, and their mouths opened with ready lasers. Metal heads turned this way and that as they clunked forward in their search. As far as Madnes could tell, there was no way out, unless a secret door had been blended in somewhere.

It wouldn't make sense not to have a door for emergency purposes, to upgrade the sentries or put out a fire or whatever else. But if it did exist, how was he going to get past those robots? One mistake, and a laser would be the last thing he ever saw.

Madnes's wrist started burning in pain and he glanced down at it. The inked clock in his skin had moved its long handle a tick.

He bit down a shout. *'I should've moved faster on my own, instead of letting the fairy take control of me!'*

Pinions tapped the side of his head.

"Uh, mister, how're we getting out of here?"

He faced a large goose eye, his own reflection staring back at him. "Oh, so you've finally realized this place is dangerous, huh? A little late, don't you think?"

Ugly blinked back at him.

Madnes sighed and shifted his attention to the sentries. *'I'm going to have to use up more of my life again, aren't I?'* Even if there was a door, no doubt there'd be trouble waiting for him on the other side of it. Best to run back up the wall, same way he'd entered. *'But can I outrun the sentries' fire power?'* That was the life-or-death question.

"I don't have a choice."

"What?" Ugly asked, his long neck cocked.

Madnes didn't bother answering. Instead, he scooped up the gray bird in one arm like a football and rose into a low crouch. Ugly honked in surprise, and robotic heads swiveled and creaked their way.

"Oh crud."

A volley of red lasers fired their way, and his legs filled with a burst of speed as the power took over him again. His body zigzagged this way and that, swerving in impossible ways and barely avoiding the hot beams streaking past them.

Alarms reverberated off the walls, rattling through his skull, and Ugly cried out just as loud. The robots moved at a creaking trot toward them.

Uh-oh, the fairy sighed. *Looks like you'll need more power than this. But it's going to cost you...*

Madnes didn't have time to think. He only knew that the power was his only way of staying alive and saving Ugly.

'Do what has to be done, then!'

But just as he thought it, a strange cry came: "Wo-uu-o-uu-o!" like something you'd hear from a jungle man. Madnes looked up. There in the sky, coming down into the compound, was a strange flying contraption—a bicycle with propellers, to be precise. And its driver grinned and gave a solute.

Some of the sentries' attention shifted to the contraption, and searing lasers flashed.

"Harrey! Watch out!!"

There was nothing Madnes could do. He ran towards the bike as it lowered, but he wasn't fast enough to reach it before the lasers made contact.

❋17❋

Going Under

R ed flashed, and Madnes desperately tried to see past the
after-glare in his vision.

Harrey, was he…?

"What, did you think we wouldn't come prepared?"

He heard his friend's voice — still alive. A pang of relief hit
Madnes. He continued in a run around the pond to reach him.
"Harrey! How did you — ? What *we*? Who's with you?"

Lasers were ricocheting off something like a curved shield.

It reflected light like a mirror, and there were two of them either side of the bike and hiding the people within. He realized with mixed emotions that Alice was in a seat behind the grinning Harrey.

At the pond's edge, Madnes leaped out over the azure surface to catch a dangling rope ladder, and quickly shimmied up one-handed, Ugly in the other.

A shield moved to give him cover until he was safely on a seat. The strange bike held several side-by-side seats; was it even a bike anymore?

"You brought Alice?" he berated him.

She glared at Madnes from the seat beside his. "I can do what I want. Don't blame Harrey. Or are you being controlling?" Her gaze narrowed.

Madnes waved his free palm defensively. "No, no, I didn't mean it like that—"

"Buckle up, troop!" Harrey grinned beneath a pair of aviator goggles as he pedaled and switched gears, making the bike ascend. Numerous lasers bounced away and then finally ceased coming. "Told you this thing worked! And I went and saved your life, haha!"

Madnes peered around a shielding mirror, while Harrey hummed pleased with his work. "Uh, Harrey?"

"Yes, passenger, sir?"

"Do you have cover for bullets?"

"Bullets?" Harrey's grin tilted. "Um...no, didn't plan that far ahead. Why?"

"We're going to be full of them in a few seconds."

"What?!"

The sentries below switched their laser mouths out for jaws full of guns.

"Oh crud."

"That's what I said earlier."

Harrey pulled on more levers. "Faster—go *faster*, bikey, me beauty! Your captain is in dire trouble!"

The bike's propellers whirred faster and faster, ascending higher and higher, and then...

K-splut-splut-spluttter...

The large top propeller sparked, slowed, and stopped spinning.

"Oh. At least we get to die together," Alice mused aloud, just before the bike dropped like a stone.

"You said this thing was fixed!!" Madnes shrieked.

"It was!"

"You said you got it working!"

"I did! It just...didn't last long!"

The contraption plummeted. They plummeted. Down, down to the watery blue depths of the pond.

SPLRssshh!

Everything went azure.

Madnes could see Alice off to his right, and Harrey a ways in front, kicking free of the bike; Ugly was still clutched in his arm, his beak wide in a silent cry.

A shimmering cold enveloped Madnes. Air. He needed air. He kicked his feet, heading towards the surface.

Why did it suddenly feel like he was going backwards?

Air. He needed air!

The surface was moving away—it was floating away from him. Why?

His legs kicked harder, his free hand paddling.

The surface's glow dimmed farther and farther away. He was sinking, and it didn't matter how much he struggled. He was being sucked down, though there was nothing pulling him.

Down...down...

Looking about, Harrey and Alice were sinking with him,

their eyes bulging and mouths screaming.

'Fairy, help us! Do something!!'

No response.

The world was nothing but an endless pure blue stretching away in every direction he turned, enveloping all of the universe. Nothing else existed.

Air!

'I can't—hold on—'

The blue turned dark as his conscious fought and failed to stay alive, sinking, sinking. There was no end, no sandy floor at the bottom of the pond.

Nothing.

Nothing but endless falling into endless blue...

❊18❊

TRANSPORTED

It came as a shock when his back brushed against something—a something without any substance, and through it he fell backwards.

Air. It was air touching his body—his back, his head, as he tried to right himself, splashing and spluttering.

How could he descend through an endless pond and find himself back up at the surface?

But there wasn't time to waste on wondering. He spotted Alice beneath the surface and caught her elbow, dragging her up to the precious air. She coughed and gulped it in.

Wrapping his free arm around hers, he kicked water and hurried her and Ugly over to shore. Bullets would be raining down on them soon—actually, they should be *already*. It didn't make sense why none had yet. Everything was eerily silent.

Pushing them up onto a grassy bank, he turned back for Harrey, only to see the guy dogpaddling towards them. "Guys? Is that you?" Harrey's aviator goggles were waterlogged, but in his panic to swim, he didn't pause to take them off, even if it meant swimming blind. Madnes caught his left wrist and tugged him up to shore.

"Take cover!" he urged the soaking wet group. But Alice remained seated on the ground and staring up at a sea-green sky.

"Alice!" Madnes moved to grab her arm, but…something felt off. A sea-green sky? He let his gaze rise to scan their surroundings.

A sky green as the sea stretched wide overhead and down to meet a hilly horizon. A field of grass spread in all directions out from the pond, rolling up to a rise of cliffs off to the left, and down to thin woods to their right. As for the pond, its surface bobbed with green and purple algae.

This wasn't the Sacred Pond. And this wasn't Oswick.

"Dude, where *are* we?" Harrey's question echoed his own thoughts.

A breeze carried salt to his nose. The ocean wasn't far off—whatever ocean it was.

Madnes snatched his hat from the pond where it bobbed, before it could get coated in algae. He had a sinking feeling.

Purple algae, sea-green sky…that didn't sound like any

place on Earth, even if he hadn't traveled every corner of the globe just yet.

Ugly coughed and honked, trying to get out the bits of water he'd breathed in from his terrible ordeal, and Madnes's attention locked onto him.

This bird...this foolish young bird that had almost got himself—and them—killed...

"Ugly, whatever gave you the idea—*of all the water sources in Oswick to choose from!*—to go to the Sacred Pond?" he nearly shouted.

The young goose jumped and trembled. "Wull...it...it sounded like a nice place, from what the crowv person told me," Ugly admitted timidly, his cheek feathers paling.

Arms akimbo, Madnes waited for Ugly to say more, but before the goose did, realization dawned on him first. "Crowv person? Did he have blond hair and gray eyes and a haughty look about him?" he asked, with an effort to keep his tone even.

Ugly's narrow head on his long neck bobbed nervously. "Uh, yeah, I think so, sir. W-why? Who was he?"

"Oz," Madnes growled. "He used you to get to me." He ran a hand aggressively through his drenched hair, top hat in his other hand. "This is the second time he's risked someone else's life to get to me..." His teeth ground together.

He had to put a stop to this! If only he knew why Oz had changed so drastically from the kind boy in his childhood memories—a kid who used to dream and find the world a fascinating place.

Madnes opened his mouth to say more when the ground beneath them suddenly tremored.

Harrey paused mid-ringing water out of his shirt and Alice ringing her skort. Another tremor came, rippling through the soil and fading away.

Madnes held out his arms for balance and scanned the field, the tree line, the cliffs.

A third tremor came, and this time Madnes could hear it as a heavy footstep. The cliffs—there was a cave there...and something coming out of it.

A deafening roar rolled over the grassy expanse, and a huge head followed by huge claw-tipped feet charged out from the cave's depths.

A monster made of purple armor scales. A dragon.

Not the cute, cuddly sort in kid's stories. No. This was a terrifying, solidly muscled and armored, and graceful creature. Grand and dangerous. You would be nothing but its plaything.

And it was charging straight at them.

"Oh *crud*. How many times am I going to have to say that today?"

Madnes swallowed, mustered his courage, and moved to intercept the dragon before it could crush his friends. But Harrey and Alice both clung to him like leeches, and Ugly sat on his head.

"What are you doing?" Madnes demanded.

"We won't let you sacrifice yourself. We either live together or die together!" shouted Alice.

"But—!" Madnes tried to shake them off. The dragon was almost upon them, its massive wings spread out like sails. "Idiots, run away! I can fight it!"

No, he couldn't. He knew he couldn't. Not unless he gave a large amount of his life to the Madness Solver power. But better that than die here, right?

"Fine, I'll tell you the truth! I was given a special power to deal with difficult situations like these. Now, let go and let me use it!"

But they wouldn't let go.

The dragon was now almost on top of them.

He could see the basketball-sized orbs for eyes, and jaws of sword teeth opening wide...

✸19✸

THE DRAGON WHO GUARDS

Asecond roar rolled out of the dragon's jaws, sending shock waves across Madnes's skin. *'Fairy, why won't you answer? Why won't you grant me power?'*

He tried to summon the power. Earlier in the compound she seemed to care. But now she was silent, indifferent in whatever corner of his mind she hid herself. He tried to think past the fear threatening to unravel him.

Warm waves of air from the dragon's breath hit the group, and the ground shook with each thunderous paw step.

They staggered backwards, ready to fall back into the pond.

Wings fanned wide and the massive, purple-scaled dragon ground to a halt—scimitar-claws stopping just shy of crushing them.

They all tipped their heads back, gaping.

The dragon's growl steamed the air, and then...

The dragon melted down.

In a writhing column of smoke, it shrunk and twisted, its shape melting and melding into something else. Once the smoke cleared, a young adult human in full armor stood in the dragon's place. Dark purplish hair fell about a face constructed of elegant sharp angles. Muscles bulged beneath scale-like armor of the same purple as the dragon's hide. He looked every inch a grand knight from fantasy tales.

Lazy jewel-like eyes roved over the group, and the dragon-man raised a hand. "You're on the grass."

Madnes blinked. "...Huh?"

As they stared wide-eyed, the young knight pointed down at their feet. "You're on the grass," he repeated.

Madnes was too shocked to understand, the fear of almost being swallowed whole by a massive dragon still shuddering his body. "So are you," he finally chirped in reply.

"Yeah, but it's my grass."

Speechless, Madnes tried to process how a dragon became a person, and now the person was telling them they were on his grass. Was this a lawn? Did dragon men have lawns?

"You're...not going to eat us, then?" he asked.

A look of barbaric disgust crossed the dragon-man's face.

"Meat? Meat is gross," his slow voice drawled. He shivered beneath his plates of armor as if Madnes had suggested something beyond comprehension. "I only ever eat greens," he stated emphatically. "Greens are good. Greens are healthy. Greens put a shine on your human skin."

"Greens?" Madnes imagined a dragon munching on a bowl of salad.

"Trees." The knight nodded over to distant woods, and sunlight caught on the tangles of his voluminous hair. "Oaks and cypress are delicious. Especially with a sprig of lemon grass and cherry ferns." He lifted his gaze dreamily, staring beyond them at whatever green meal his imagination must be brewing up.

Madnes felt Harrey and Alice slowly let their hold on him relax. Ugly cocked his bird head to one side, and Madnes to the other side. They waited until the dragon-man snapped out of his daydream.

A gauntleted hand waved. "You're still on the grass."

"Oh." They all shuffled backwards. A dirt path circled the pond—they stood on that.

The knight cocked his head at a lazy angle, glittering eyes regarding each of them. "Where are you from? Nobody that's nobody nears my cave," he drawled.

"Nobody that's what?" Madnes shook his confused head.

Harrey piped up behind him, "I think first we gotta know *where* we are?"

That was the first logical thing Harrey had said in a long time. "Apparently there are dragons here, so I'm thinking maybe...Norway?"

And that was the dumbest thing Harrey had said in a long time.

The dragon knight eyed Harrey, very perplexed. "What is a Norway?"

Madnes slapped a hand over Harrey's mouth before he could answer, and asked instead, "We're in Wonderland, aren't we?"

The knight nodded.

Harrey's eyes bugged out as far as they could go, and Alice gazed around her with newfound wonder.

"That pond, it's linked to our world?" Madnes surmised, combing a strand of hair behind his ear. "That explains the old legend, and why people thought the pond was sacred. Long ago, something from Wonderland must have come through. But I thought few Earthians could see Wonderlanders who cross over?"

"This is the portal that I guard," the knight stated, either ignoring or ignorant of what he had just said. Madnes squinted; it was probably the latter.

"Whoa, whoa, wait you guys." Harrey's hand caught the edge of his sleeve, tugging Madnes around to face him. "Wonderland? Did I hear what I thought I just heard? This isn't some dream I'm having after eating half a pizza last night, right?"

"You said you have a special power?" Alice came at Madnes from the other side, her fists planted on her hips. "You've got some explaining to do, Madnes Hatter."

Sweat beaded Madnes's temples. "Ah, yeah. I guess now that you're in *their* world, you can see them," he half said to himself, then cleared his throat. "Welcome to Wonderland, I guess." He gestured with a sweep of an arm.

❈20❈
WELCOME TO
WONDERLAND

Cheshire flipped open book after old book, page after yellowed page, scouring the Red Palace's library in Wonderland—in search of words, hints, *anything* that could tell him where the Madness Solver power originated from and how it all began.

The clues must be there somewhere, clues that could save Madnes from the power before it was too late. If only he could locate the information…

"Why, Cheshire, what brings you here?" spoke a voice at his back.

Cheshire turned around, tipping his head far back to meet Oz's gaze.

"Prince Oz, what a coincidence meeting you here." He gave a formal bow, to which Oz slightly inclined his head.

"I am often in the library. I'm surprised you didn't know I was once a voracious reader."

"Haha, my mistake." Cheshire grinned sheepishly. "I'm doing a little research into the ancient history of Wonderland. In particular the history of the Madness Solver. You wouldn't happen to know of any old—perhaps hidden away—books on the subject, would you?"

"Hmm." Oz tapped his fingers on his hip and looked to the ceiling in thought. "Other than what we have in the regular history books, can't say that I've come across anything. What was recorded about the first Madness Solver isn't much." He flashed an apologetic smile. "Sorry I can't be of more help, Cheshire."

The cat heaved a sigh. "No, no. That's quite all right. I knew this would be a difficult task from the start." He brushed at his whiskers and looked back to the rows of books lining the three-level royal library. "Maybe…could you direct me to the mythological and folklore section?"

Oz gave a nod and led the way, his blue cape swishing. He stopped at a bookcase tucked into an alcove, gesturing toward it with a palm. "Our oldest collection of myths, legends and whatnot, Cheshire."

"Thank you, Your Highness."

A half smile tweaked Oz's lips. "I have other matters to

attend today, so I'll be taking my leave now."

"Yes, yes, of course." Cheshire bowed as the prince left his presence, cape sweeping the marble floor behind him.

It was no easy task explaining Wonderland, the mysterious power, and his new job to his bewildered friends. Madnes's face felt drenched in sweat by the time he finished.

He left out the most important fact, however: that his life was the price paid for using the power. Every time he used it, the clock on his wrist ticked away at his life. He wasn't allowed to tell them—that was one of the rules. Who knew what would happen if he broke it?

"Ohhh." Realization dawned on Harrey's face. "That's why you were talking to air and paper bags n' other weird stuff. Those were Wonderlanders in disguise. You weren't just going crazy."

"Yes, I'm not crazy, thank you," said Madnes with a frown. "Not yet, anyway…"

"You could have told us from the start, Madnes," said Alice, trying not to pout. He cocked an eyebrow. She exhaled loudly. "*Fine.* It would've sounded crazy, and most likely we wouldn't have believed you—something as impossible as this."

"Thanks for understanding," he told her. "There were a few times when I wanted to say, but…I couldn't get the right words out."

She nodded knowingly.

A beam of sunlight caught in Alice's hair, and for a moment it wasn't just blonde but glowing like golden flames. Madness's jaw fell slack. But when he blinked and looked again, she appeared normal, nothing out of the ordinary.

Alice's eyebrows drew together and she shrugged with a question, as if wondering why he was staring at her.

Madnes opened and closed his mouth, shook his head and diverted his attention elsewhere, patting Ugly as the goose perched on his shoulder.

Armor creaked and the dragon knight, who had been waiting patiently all this time, raised a hand lazily to interrupt the group's chatter. "Are you planning on living here?" he asked them.

"What? No, no. We'll leave your grass, yard, living space or whatever it is. But we can't go back home the same way we came—not unless we want to meet our end in the Sacred Pond's waters." Madnes combed a hand through his drying hair. "Is there another way to Oswick?"

The dragon knight nodded. "There are a few other portals," he drawled. "It will be faster if I take you there, Madness Solver." His head inclined. "Pardon for my earlier ignorance in not recognizing you for who you are."

Madnes waved his hands that all was fine. "You help guard the portals I'm supposed to manage. In a way, we're sort of colleagues."

The knight blushed lazily. "You honor me, Sir Madnes."

"Do you have a name?"

"I am the purple knight."

"...Yes, you are a knight with purple armor, who becomes a purple dragon. I get that. But your name?"

"Purple dragon knight."

Madnes stared at him levelly. "Do dragons not have names?"

The knight tilted his head.

Madnes sighed. "We'll get nowhere with this, will we? How about this: I come up with a name for you using *purple*."

The knight's face perked, suddenly intrigued.

"Oo-oo! A game! Let me play!" Harrey chimed in. "Pleur! Prepul? Lepur. Purlep? Pelrup?"

Madnes rubbed his forehead. "How about Pelur?" he said, before Harrey could continue. "We'll call you Knight Pelur. How's that?"

Stars sparkled in the knight's eyes. "A true name. My life has meaning."

"Eh…didn't it have meaning before?" Madnes stalled his reply with a raised hand. "Anyways, will you take us to the portal now?"

Pelur dipped his head, dark purple hair falling forward. "It's after lunchtime, but I'll manage. For you, Sir Madnes."

"Um, thank you."

A swirl of smoke lifted from the ground around the knight as he backed away, obscuring him from view, and a deep growl rumbled the ground.

They took cautionary steps back, and a hot breath of air cleared the smoke away in one giant puff—almost clearing Madnes and the group away in the process.

There stood the fearsome dragon in Pelur's place. He swept a webbed wing down for them to climb onto his back.

They tried to find a seat, avoiding the long, curved spikes that lined Pelur's spine. It worked better sitting sideways and using the spikes as safety bars—something to cling to as the massive dragon shifted, stood on hide legs, and launched into the air with all the force of a giant spring.

"*Gwaaah!*" Harrey's mouth flapped wildly in the rush of air, and Alice's arms found their way around Madnes's chest, clinging tightly—he blushed and didn't mind.

Once the dragon leveled out in the air, things calmed down, and they could peer over Pelur's sides down at Wonderland below.

The coast was under them, a sea of blue crashing upon colorfully striped cliffs. The portal and Pelur's cave lay situated on a jut of land attached to the mainland by a narrow strip, which they soon left behind, coming over a landscape so bizarre that no sense could be made of it.

It was beautiful. It was mysterious. Colors painted portions of Wonderland like a canvas, while other portions simmered dark and secretive. In the rolling landscape's center rose a castle. Red as blood, its towers and domes reached for the sky in gothic wonder.

"The Red King's palace," rumbled dragon Pelur.

Madnes focused on the palace as they drew nearer and nearer. He squinted against the wind. "Oz, so this is where you've been living? All this time?" he whispered.

Cheshire crossed the blue-green lawn as he exited the palace library. An odd smudge up in the sky caught his attention.

Shielding against the sun with a paw, he spotted the purple dragon.

And on the dragon was...

"Madnes? Alice *and* Harrey?!"

❖21❖

CONFRONTATION

"What in Wonderland is going on?" Cheshire exclaimed, once dragon Pelur had landed on a patch of ground near the palace, the trees and soil trembling underpaw.

The cat eyed the gosling perched on Madnes's shoulder. "Do I *want* to know what happened since I left? Do I *want* to know what Harrey and Alice are doing here, in the first place?"

"Um...probably not." Madnes chewed his thumb nail, glancing away.

"Stop chewing your nail—that's a bad habit," ordered Cheshire. Madnes lowered his thumb. "So, you brought Earthians to Wonderland," the cat stated with an accusing tone. "Did I not warn you that our world must be kept a secret?"

Madnes crossed his arms. "There are humans—*erm*, Earthians—who know about Wonderland already. You've said so."

"Yes, a very select few—and them mostly by accident." Cheshire's furry brow creased. "I understand that they're your closest friends, and that it's difficult keeping secrets from them. But now that they've seen Wonderland, their lives back on Earth won't be the same."

Madnes glanced down at the grass.

"Hey now, there's no reason to be upset," Harrey interjected. "I'm glad I know! This place is awesome!" He hooked an arm around Madnes's neck playfully, and Ugly flapped out of the way, honking. "Plus, we get to help support our buddy in his *world peacekeeping* job, now."

The cat huffed, still irked, tail twitching.

A loud ripping sound brought their heads around to see Pelur's large paw grab and yank up tree after tree, stuffing the leafy tops into his jaws and munching like a human would on celery.

"Purple dragon!" Cheshire waved pleading paws. "Please mind the palace grounds—those trees are not meant for eating!"

"It's Pelur, now, Sir Cheshire."

"Pardon?"

"Sir Madnes gave me a proper name." The dragon flashed a sleepy grin that showed many pointy teeth.

The cat gave him a look and Madnes shrugged nonchalantly.

Cheshire rubbed his paw over his brow. "We'll discuss this more, later. But now that you're here…" He pulled out a large book from the crook of his small arm. "I did some research, as I said I would, and I found some curious—"

"So fluffy!"

Cheshire was suddenly whisked up into arms and held against a human face and chest, as Alice picked him up and hugged him.

"M-miss! Please—restrain yourself! I'm losing my dignity!"

He heard Madnes snicker and glared in his direction. Madnes covered his mouth with a hand and pretended to whistle.

"Sorry, Cheshire." Alice stroked the soft cat fur peeking out from his suit vest before reluctantly releasing him. "I can't resist cute animals, especially ones that play dress-up."

"I don't play dress up," he tried to say. He straightened his bowtie and once more lifted the book and plopped it into Madnes's hands.

Munch, munch.

"Stop eating those trees! *Oh no*, you've gone and ruined the royal orchid patch too," the cat moaned.

"Orchids are bitter. I wondered what that taste was," drawled Pelur.

"Stop eating them, then! Those are prized orchids!"

Madnes hefted the book. It was heavy and leather, and had a painting stamped on the cover: a woman bursting from a pool of water, with flowing green hair and fairy-like wings. "*Tales & Mythology.* You think the answer lies in here?"

Cheshire turned from berating the dragon. "More of a guess," he admitted. "An answer to a question, though not to all of them."

A dark speck moved across the sky, making Madnes look up from the tabby cat.

Flying overhead from the palace was a person—a person with large black wings. Wings like a crow.

"Oz!"

The prince hadn't spotted him yet. Now was his chance!

Madnes broke into a run after him, as the prince drifted higher and higher. Gathering speed and momentum, and using just a touch of power, he caught up to Oz from below, and then—with one giant, knee-bursting leap—he launched himself into the air, hands outstretched to catch Oz by the ankles.

The sudden grab and extra weight caught Oz by surprise.

"I've got a few bones to pick with you, Oz! We're gonna have a talk, just you and me!" shouted Madnes.

Oz's eyes went wide for a second, no doubt shocked that someone had caught him mid-flight—and that that someone was Madnes, here in Wonderland.

"Madnes!" Cheshire screeched from the ground, waving his arms in a panic. "What in blazes are you doing? That's the prince you're assaulting!"

"Fight! Fight!" Harrey chanted. "Wait a minute, Oz is a *prince* here?" The exuberant boy gaped, then he shouted, "Kick his princely hindquarters, Madnes!!"

"Stop encouraging him!" Cheshire reprimanded. But something in Harrey's words made him pause. "Hold on, do you *know* Oz?"

"He and Madnes used to be besties when they were kids," Harrey said. "What, you didn't know?"

Madnes battled to keep his grip on Oz's ankles while the prince kicked, dove, and spiraled through the air.

"Have a talk with you? As if," Oz snarled. Blue cape flapping in the wind, he reached down and grabbed one of Madnes's arms to yank it off. But Madnes was stronger than he used to be, and he clung to him in a tight grip.

"I understand if you hate me, resent me," Madnes shouted against the rushing air as they flew, "but you put Alice's life in danger, and then Ugly Duckling's. I can't so easily forgive that, Oz!"

"I'm not seeking your forgiveness." Oz's hand morphed into crow talons digging into his arm. Madnes bit down a yelp. "If you weren't so pathetic and inadequate at using that power, you would have sensed the danger in time and stopped me!"

Madnes opened his mouth to shout back, but nothing came out.

Yes, he was inadequate; he'd known that from the start. But even so...

"It wasn't *my* fault that the power wanted me instead of you. So stop being a selfish crybaby about it!" Madnes finally said.

Oz's jaw dropped. "Selfish *what*?" In all his life, nobody had ever dared say such a thing! No, that wasn't true. During his time on Earth, bullies had said plenty, and it was child Madnes who had chased them off—Madnes who used to mean the world to him.

"You are lower than a worm," Oz growled. "Traitors like you deserve every pain the worlds have to offer!"

"I didn't betray you! It wasn't like that—" Madnes tried to say.

Claws dug deeper, and the pain made Madnes's hand jerk back involuntarily.

Oz seized the moment, taloned hands grabbing both Madnes's wrists in a grip that drew blood and finally yanked

Madnes free of his ankles. Oz then flapped his wings into a spin—spinning Madnes round and round, before throwing him with all his might.

Madnes flung away like a ragdoll across the sky, disappearing into the tree-lined horizon.

❋22❋
THAT DISTANT MEMORY

"Think you're fancy because you've got nice clothes, do you?"

"You rich types don't belong in Oswick."

"Get lost. We don't want you here!"

Three boys surrounded a child: a blond boy, clutching a book to his chest as if it could save him from their taunts.

"What's that book you've got there?" One reached to steal it away.

The child turned, blocking with his back, but another boy yanked the book free from his arms.

"No! Give it back!"

"Likes to read, does he?" The second bully dangled the book just out of reach. "I bet he does it to make himself feel smarter than everybody else. *Heheh*, we should beat that pride out of you."

"I don't! Please." Tears rolled down the child's cheeks. "It's just a book. Give it back!"

A fist to the stomach brought him to his knees, gasping for air. The child resisted the urge to clutch his painful belly and instead covered his head protectively, knowing more blows would come.

He waited for the pain to begin.

"Oi!"

The three older boys turned at a shout, and child Oz peeked from under his shielding arms.

A boy with a quirky top hat approached, not much taller than himself, with violet eyes that now blazed anger.

"Give that book back, and go do something useful with your lives. I'm not gonna let bullies do as they please!"

"Huh?" The bully with the book made a rude face at him. "Why the heck would we listen to you?"

A fist suddenly knocked the older kid down, and the top hat boy moved faster than any of them could follow. He snatched up the fallen book and grabbed Oz by the wrist, pulling him into a run with him.

Together, they fled the scene before the bullies could recover their wits.

The strange boy laughed, glancing at the finely dressed Oz who he pulled in tow. "You're new around here, aren't you? You can stick with me, if you like!"

Oz's mouth hung open, his legs struggling to keep up. Something inside him lit up with newfound hope. "Y-yes, I would like that. I'm Oz," he said between breaths. "Who are you?"

The boy grinned back at him. "Madnes Hatter!"

The Present

Pain. His arms. Madnes forced his eyelids to open and see the cause—then he regretted the effort as a headache split his head in two. Groggy and feeling like he'd been hit by a truck, he let his eyes drift closed again. He recalled being flung mercilessly through the air, the sensation of falling.

'Where am I?'

The ghost image of a blond child smiled in his mind.

"Oz!" Madnes reached out with a shout, grasping for that image, that distant memory.

A loud snapping noise woke his senses, and the image vanished. Taking in a breath, he carefully shifted his torso and glanced about to find that his body was sprawled across a tangle of branches many stories above the ground.

A flashback recalled his fight with Oz, how he fell through sky and into a swath of dangling blue vines. A group of miniature purple monkeys watched him curiously now through the canopy.

'I can't move. Every part of me aches…'

Stupid human. You forced me to heal you, or else you'd be an invalid with a broken spine by now. A familiar voice spoke inside his head: the fairy of the Madness Solver power.

That healing cost you a bit of life, just so you know. Her elfin face spoke haughtily. *Tick-tock!* Her arm motioned the ticking movement of a clock's hand.

His wrist. He didn't dare look at the inked clock on his skin. Whether it was months or a year of life lost, he didn't want to know.

'You've been silent all this time, fairy. Why?' he demanded, barely keeping his anger in check.

Hm. She shrugged white opal shoulders. *You didn't need me. You just thought you did. And besides, it was entertaining to watch.* A giggle echoed through his head.

"More like an evil imp than a fairy..." Madnes muttered under his breath.

Voices were calling out. He could hear people searching for him, and a wash of relief swept through. It wasn't long before Pelur's dragon claw lifted him out of the tangled vine canopy—attempting to do so gently, but quite a few twigs and vines still slapped Madnes in the face. He was soon set on the blessed ground and felt Alice's comforting embrace around his neck.

"Dude, you gotta be smarter when facing Oz. He's tough!" Harrey slapped his shoulder. "You sure went soaring like a rocket! Must've been one heck of a flight, eh?"

Madnes didn't have the energy to respond.

Paws shoved Harrey and Alice aside. "You should have told me about this, Madnes! I had no idea things were so bitter between you and Oz." Cheshire's furious cat face filled his vision and he winced. "How am I supposed to help you when you're keeping secrets from me?"

Madnes looked away. Alice held out his top hat for him, having found it, and he patted the hat securely on his head. "I didn't think it was relevant. I'm sorry, okay?"

Cheshire huffed but relented. "It's getting late," he said. "We can't stay here in the woods."

They looked around at the pressing trees and curling blue vines, purple monkey eyes peeking out at them from every crevice. The fading light made Madnes wonder what night was like in Wonderland.

"Where did Oz go? I'm not done knocking sense into his brain yet."

Harrey guffawed. "Who knows? Princely duties and new evil schemes, probably."

A paw motioned at them, "Come on, I'll take you to my place for some refreshments." The cat patted the leather book hooked under his arm. "And I'll tell you an interesting old tale I found."

At the edge of the woods, close to a village, sat Cheshire's cottage. A quaint little house with a vegetable and flower garden, and a white-picket fence.

"It's like a fantasy cottage," swooned Alice.

"Yeah, a real shocker."

Cheshire unlocked the wooden arched door and eyed Madnes. "What's that supposed to mean?"

Madnes smirked. "It's not a giant mushroom or something else ridiculous."

Cheshire rolled his eyes and let them inside the polished wood interior.

Soon, a pot of tea was set on a tablecloth, and cups shaped like tulips were served. The group took seats around a small table, and Ugly Duckling busied himself with a biscuit.

"Now then." The cat sighed after taking a deep, calming sip of spicy tea. "Now that we're all settled, let me share with you a tale I found in this book of mythology…"

❋23❋

LEGEND OF THE

NYMPHS

"*Once upon a time, there was a nymph who loved to explore. She was a powerful creature among her kind, and very inquisitive. To feed her adventurous spirit, every day she journeyed through Wonderland's many portals opened to other worlds, investigating what lay beyond each watery door.*

One day, she came upon a portal in the shape and form of a pond. She dived through its waters and resurfaced into another world. Sunlight slanted through wide leaves and trees. Everything was green and lush, the sky painted blue. This new world's atmosphere dazzled her.

"Help...me..."

The nymph heard a pitiful sound, a croak from a dying voice.

There, on the grassy bank before her, was a boy crawling desperately on his knees and flesh-eaten hands toward the water.

So horrid was his state that she gasped in shock and rushed forward to meet him at the water's edge. A terrible plague had taken hold of him, the nymph surmised. She ignored her fear and the warnings in the back of her mind, and reached out to him as he moaned and sobbed, touching his left hand.

Power flowed from her into him—eradicating the disease and healing his body.

The boy leaned back on his knees, raised both palms and inspected them with a look of wonder and awe. His body was healthy again, and he looked across at the nymph.

She did not know what sort of creature he was, but she felt glad to have ended his pain. Before he could come any closer or ask questions, however, she dove back under the surface and returned to Wonderland.

The moment she touched the air and was reunited with her beloved home world, she felt something inside her unbalance. Days passed, and the feeling in her grew worse. Her dreams turned to nightmares, and her once lovely wings grew dark and her eyes venomous. The very air she breathed turned black, and it wasn't long after that that the nymph died.

Those around her saw what had happened. As she died, a darkness seeped out of her body—a black fog that churned like a living thing and spread across the land. A darkness that Wonderlanders have since named Syn.

Touching the human boy had contracted in her a darkness common to Earth but unknown to Wonderland. By the nymph's foolish actions, Syn contaminated the lands and peoples, and Wonderland was forever changed from being a place of peace and harmony to a place of strife and selfish greed, ever since that day.

The nymphs bore the punishment for this from then on. A foolish race, they were hated and hunted down for their crime of bringing this darkness into their world. For who knew what next the nymphs might bring with them into Wonderland? After many years of persecution, their kind was wiped out.

No longer do the ignorant nymphs roam the world. And as they were exterminated, much of Syn vanished with them—though not all of it. Wonderland would never be the same peaceful place again.

Beware, young children and those foolish of heart, for you never know what might be lurking nearby in the shadows. Syn preys upon the weak and ignorant. Beware. You never know when Syn will creep near and strike your unguarded mind..."

Cheshire set the old book down, finished reading the grim legend from its worn pages.

From his seat, Harrey gawked. "Wow. And I thought Earth had creepy legends."

Cheshire sipped tea from his porcelain tulip cup. "I remember the *Tale of Syn*. My mother used to tell it to me, saying that Syn would come and take me away if I didn't behave. That used to scare the wits out of me." The cat chuckled through his whiskers.

"All humans have it?" asked Madnes, seated next to him.

"It's been said that all Earthians do, yes—to some degree— if you believe such a tale. It's the darkness that urges a person to do terrible things, a consuming and selfish evil. And it found its way into Wonderland long ago, according to this."

'Could something like that have happened to Oz?' Madnes wondered. He rested his elbows on the table, folded hands propping up his chin. "Does it really affect Wonderlanders differently than Earthians?"

"I'd think it would depend on each person individually," replied Cheshire. "But if Syn is real, and is here, then I suppose we're all infected in some way already. No one much worries about it anymore, though. Wonderlanders love to visit Earth."

"Hmm." The drastic change in Oz, who once lived among humans for a time…could that dark illness be the culprit? He needed evidence. He needed to investigate the truth about this mysterious Syn.

"This resembles our story about the Sacred Pond," Madnes recollected, turning the tale over in his mind, analyzing the pieces.

"Quite right. Though, my point is that this fairy person you describe to be in your head sounds similar to these nymphs who no longer exist. I'm not sure about the tale itself, but the part about hunting down nymphs to extinction is true. I came across much evidence for that during my research," Cheshire confirmed.

"Nymphs, huh. That tale sounds like a big blame game to me—a reason to get rid of their kind," said Madnes.

"I agree it's a sad and wrong thing that happened. Powerful creatures are often feared or coveted."

"So, you couldn't find anything about the first Madness Solver, or what the power even is? There's nothing but bits and scraps about Wonderland's ancient history? Don't you find that odd?" The wheels in Madnes's mind turned, unable to resist working at the mystery puzzle before him. "An entire race wiped out…"

Something stirred deep inside his subconscious: thoughts from the fairy herself. Too subtle to read, but he could feel a jumble of emotions and something screaming of hate.

"Sounds like someone important in Wonderland is keeping a secret."

"Who? You mean the king?" Cheshire went wide-eyed. Madnes leaned back in his chair and folded his arms. "Madnes, that's treacherous talk! You can't just blame the king—not without concrete evidence!" Cheshire lowered his voice. "Why would he create such a lie? What reason would he have? You'd better get your facts straight before accusing someone powerful like him."

"*Hmph*, I don't know if it was him or a previous ruler, or some creepy old mage hiding under a rock. But somebody—somewhere—is keeping the past a secret. That's what my Madness Solver gut is telling me, anyway."

Cheshire's nose twitched and he busied himself taking another sip of tea. Perhaps the thought of Wonderland's great ruler being a liar was too much to consider. Madnes exhaled and let the gears spinning inside his brain cool down.

"So, if the power is one of these nymphs—a last survivor—then how does knowing that…" he leaned to the cat's twitching ear, whispering so the others couldn't hear, "…keep it from taking my life?"

"Ah, well, I don't know that bit yet. But one thing at a time, Madnes. Step one to solving any problem is to first know what it is you're dealing with."

"Okay. And step two is stopping it from sipping me away as you are that cup of tea?"

"To find a *different* energy source for the creature to consume, yes," Cheshire corrected with emphasis. "But the power cannot be taken out of you, if that's what you're hoping, Madnes. We need the Madness Solver. The power must always exist and be available for use—as I've explained to you before. A necessary, if painful, truth." He eyed him thoughtfully. "Especially if what your gut is telling you is true."

"Yeah, yeah, I get it." Madnes waved a hand.

Beyond the round window frames of the cottage, evening shifted to dusk with a blood moon slowly waltzing its way up the sky, the craters marring its surface forming a creepy smile down at the world below.

"My mom's going to tear me to shreds when I don't show up home tonight…"

❄24❄

ℙEEPER

The Madness Solver fairy…a possible last survivor of the race of nymphs, who had been made extinct long ago…

It was an intriguing mystery, and one Madnes had to solve if he wanted a lifespan longer than a chipmunk's. He doubted the fairy would respond if he tried asking about it, though. She seemed quite content to keep things to herself and be of no help. She probably wouldn't even tell him if the dark Syn was a real thing or not, and if it still lurked Wonderland as the legend told.

Madnes rose from the chair to stretch his legs. "I'm going out for some fresh air."

"I wouldn't recommend it," called Cheshire. His paws padded to the kitchen sink and he began washing teacups.

Madnes paused, hand on the doorknob, almost tempted to open the door without listening. "Do I dare ask why not? What's out there in Wonderland at night?"

"Many things." Cheshire looked to the ceiling, as if there were too many to name. "But around this time of year, there will be vampire frogs about."

Madnes face-palmed. "Vampire frogs? Why am I not surprised... I'll swat them away, then, if that's the case."

"I wouldn't go outside and tempt them, if I were you, Madnes," the cat warned, though he made no move to stop him.

With a huff, Madnes chose to ignore caution and opened the door, stepping out into the night. Cool fresh air blew across him, and he soaked it in gratefully. A dull, pear-shaped porchlight cast a circle of light around him.

It was nice out here. Peaceful.

"Vampire frogs," he muttered, disbelieving. He rubbed his aching arms, still soar even if healed after his ordeal with Oz. "What's so scary about a frog with fangs? *Heh*, it's humans with fangs that I'd be more afraid of..."

Hop.

Something plopped from beyond the shadows.

Madnes whirled around but couldn't see anything.

"It's nothing, it's nothing." He slapped his cheeks to make sure he was awake. The creepy moon was grinning down at him, unsettling his nerves.

"I'm just overreacting."

Hop.

Something landed just beyond the porchlight's reach.

He peered, trying to see through the darkness.

Twin large round eyes glowed from the shadows, reflecting the faint light. The eyeballs stared up at him, unblinking and red, and a brown frog slowly crawled into view.

Madnes swallowed, shook his head, then stared threateningly back at the small creature. "I refuse to feel threatened by a frog."

Hop.

It stared…

Hop.

It inched closer…

Madnes's legs trembled and his lips twitched.

Hop.

The frog's mouth opened, dark and wide, and twin fangs slid out. A herd of hopping frogs joined in from the darkness. And then, as one, they leaped—high up at his face.

"*YEEK!*" Madnes's fists shot out, punching the frogs away, and he bolted back inside the cottage.

"Back already?" Cheshire asked with the hint of a smirk.

Madnes turned his nose away, refusing to justify that smirk. "I'm off to bed," he said tightly and marched over to a sofa. Vampire frogs would scar his dreams tonight.

'I'll never look at a frog the same way again.'

Dappled light tickled behind Madnes's eyelids until he opened them and sat up from the makeshift sofa-bed. It was still early dawn.

Harrey was sound asleep, drooling over a sofa chair; Ugly had made a nest in his hair, his snore a wheezing hiss.

Cheshire must be snug in his own kitty room. And Alice…where *was* Alice?

Madnes eased open the door quietly, peeking his head out first—not because he was afraid of vampire amphibians or anything, but just to be on the safe side.

A loud *munch* startled him out of his boots, and he had to clamp his mouth shut not to yelp.

Pelur was eating a massive head of lettuce, munching loudly on it, in his human form by the doorstep. He lazily looked sideways at Madnes. "Want one?"

"Ah, no. None whatsoever," Madnes kindly dodged the offer. "Have you seen Alice?"

Pelur paused mid munch to tilt his head, looking up at the clouds and thinking. "Hm. Yes. Yes, I did."

Madnes waited for more than that, but nothing came, and he realized with a groan that if he didn't ask specifics, Pelur was too slow in the head to think to give any details. "And? Where is she?"

A gauntleted hand pointed to the back of the house, beyond a patch of woods there.

"Thanks."

Madnes trotted off and, reaching the woods, made his way around trunks and hanging moss. "What does she think she's doing, wandering all the way out here on her own in a strange world?" he mumbled. "No telling what kind of fanged creatures might lurk about…"

The trees parted up ahead, and the soft light of dawn reflected on a small pool of water—perfectly round and clean, with rising trails of steam.

He was about to venture near, when the light patter of footsteps made him duck behind the nearest tree.

It was Alice, and wearing a towel around her.

Puzzled, he peeked around the bark, careful not to let her see him. There was something odd about her lately—a wild look in her sea-green eyes, an unnatural glow to her hair and skin. Maybe if he watched, he could find out why.

Her back turned to him as she faced the steaming pool. With a sudden blush, he realized what she was there to do and quickly looked away—or would have, if not for a strange, unearthly glow that suddenly enveloped her.

As she stepped into the pool, light illumined her. No—it was coming *from* her; she *was* the light. Her skin glowed like liquid sunlight, blending into the dawn's golden rays.

Peeking one eye around the tree, he half-watched, dumbstruck by the transformation. Her glowing form dove into the water and was gone.

Minutes passed…and she did not resurface.

"Alice?" Fearing the worst, he dashed over to the pool's edge.

His eyes scanned but couldn't find her amidst the dappled light playing across the pool's surface.

Heart thumping wildly, he bent down to the water and prepared to dive in.

A fist suddenly shot out from the surface, just then, and grazed his right cheek.

"PEEPING TOM!"

"What?!"

Alice resurfaced with a loud splash, her face red with fury.

A yelp caught in his throat and he toppled backwards onto his backside. "Alice! Wait! I wasn't—didn't mean to—"

He realized how the situation must look. Her skin was no longer glowing; she looked nothing different from the Alice he knew.

"Oh crud."

WHAM!

She had a fierce kick for a petite person. Towel wrapped around her, she punched and kicked and slapped the stars out of his head.

He fell like a log to the ground, bruised eyelids twitching.

"You're here to peek?" a goose squawked shrilly.

He glimpsed Ugly and Knight Pelur appearing on the scene.

"Shame on you, Madness Solver! How indecent!!" Feathers slapped at him. "How can my feathers take their turn at the bath with you peeping around?"

"Peeping?" Pelur made an unmanly squeal, hands moving to shield his body from view as if Madnes could see through the layers of armor the guy wore.

"I w-wsn't..." Madnes's bruised lips gurgled.

They continued to squeal and slap, and he struggled to crawl away.

Forget the vampire frog nightmare—this was going to leave a bigger scar.

✦25✦

ℛETURNING ℋOME

Madnes found himself near the palace grounds once again as Cheshire led their group to the nearest portal connected to Oswick.

Alice had been silent the whole way. And for a while, Ugly and Pelur muttered about how indecent Madnes was. Harrey laughed his head off like it was the greatest joke ever, and Cheshire shook his furry head now and then.

Madnes pulled the brim of his hat down over his face, wishing that all of him could disappear inside it.

The image of Alice, her skin glowing like the molten sun, flashed through his mind. *'Who is Alice really?'*

He'd known her for years—or thought he had—a normal girl moved to Oswick. But now, he wasn't so sure if she was even from Earth.

'All this time she acted like she couldn't see Wonderlanders... Was it a lie?'

Had she known of Wonderland and the Madness Solver power all along?

'But why would she keep it secret from me?'

So many questions...if only he could find the right time and place to ask them. Problem was, asking anything about her appearance at the pond would bring up the "peeping tom" incident—and he really didn't want to bring that back up, nor give her more reason to bash his head in.

'First Oz, then the mystery of nymphs, and now this!' He clawed at his aching head, his brain feeling like an overloaded water balloon ready to burst. Too many mysteries—were they all connected or not? He needed a break. But none would come anytime soon; there were things to sort out today.

Cheshire halted and stepped aside before two metal trees, their thick trunks bowed and forming the frame of an archway between them. The surface swirled like moving water.

"The portal," the cat introduced, indicating the arch.

"I guess this is goodbye," Knight Pelur drawled to the group. "It's been fun, a very nice and not-boring time. Do visit again."

"Ah, sure. We'll have to keep in touch," said Madnes, shaking one gauntleted hand, Harrey shaking the other.

"You're the coolest, bud. I'm gonna miss you! You gotta visit Oswick some time." Harrey beamed.

"Um, not as a dragon, though," Madnes added.

"Sir Madnes?" Ugly honked. "You won't tell my mom about all this—the Sacred Pond and all—will you?"

Madnes wiped his brow; just thinking about that goose woman made him weary. "I won't, if you won't."

The last thing he wanted was her shrieking down his ear about Ugly nearly becoming a fried goose.

"Hurry on, hurry on. Best not dawdle," urged Cheshire.

Alice went through first, marching with a hurried step before anyone else could.

Harrey elbowed Madnes. "Yikes, she's never gonna forgive you."

Madnes flashed Harrey a scowl before following through the arch portal and back into Oswick.

"Well, it's about time!"

Mother Goose marched—or rather, waddled—toward the park bench where Madnes, Harrey and Cheshire sat waiting with Ugly Duckling. Her red-rimmed glasses glinted beneath her pristine white bonnet.

Harrey had to blink twice at the impeccably dressed goose—his first time seeing Wonderlanders on Earth, now that the trip had made him able to see; and he was gawking rudely.

Ugly dipped his head nervously, and it was with great slowness that he hopped down off the bench to meet his mother.

"I've been worried sick, waiting without hearing any news from you people!" Mother Goose hissed at them. Her wing caught Ugly and pulled him close. "Incompetent! Careless! I could have done a better job myself."

Any bit of guilt he'd had for causing her worry vanished, and Madnes readied to snap back that maybe she *should've* gone and looked for him herself. But Cheshire's paw on his wrist stopped him.

"We do apologize, Madam Mother Goose," Cheshire soothed. "There were unforeseen circumstances which interfered with our contacting you. But I assure you that Ugly has been safe with us since we found him yesterday."

"*Hmph!* I should hope so. But an excuse is no excuse for lazy work. And as for you," she turned Ugly around to face her. "Running off like that, really! How many age wrinkles will I suffer now because of you?" she snapped. "Don't think you'll be stepping one foot out the door this month—you're grounded! And I'll not have you go anywhere without adult supervision from now on. Is that clear?"

Ugly hung his long neck and head miserably.

Madnes couldn't stand it any longer. "He wouldn't have run off if you weren't such a strict, unpleasant person to be around!"

Harrey covered a gasp with both hands, and Cheshire's furry eyebrows drew down. "Madnes—" he started.

But Madnes's hand halted the cat. "No, it's the truth, and we all know it. It's about time someone told you, Mother Goose. Your behavior is what drove Ugly to run away. Can't you see what you're doing? Is this really how you want to raise him? Do you want Ugly to resent you when he grows up and leaves home? This is nothing but a recipe for a miserable family—one that won't care about you when you're old and gray and in need. So, think about that."

Finished with his rant, Madnes wiped his forehead and prepared for the worst. Everybody was cringing.

But he noticed the goose woman's round eyes staring widely up at him over the glasses.

She gave a shake to Ugly's shoulders and he sheepishly looked at her. "Is that how you see me, Ugly?" she asked.

Her son didn't answer.

"But a mother should be strict, and she cannot always be a pleasant person because of it."

"I know," Ugly plucked up some courage to say. "B-but you could be more aware of my feelings and care a little. We never do anything fun together, either." Sunlight caught on a tear.

"...Oh." She released her hold on him. "I see... Well, it wasn't my intention to be so...unaware. I'm just so busy making this place our home." Was that a sniffle in Mother Goose's beak? "Maybe we could spend some time together doing things outside of school and work. I suppose a child your age should have other gosling friends to play with, as well..." She straightened. "We'll have to work on that."

"Really?" Ugly brightened, then hopped up and hugged his wings around her.

"Oh, oh my." Mother caught her balance, taken by surprise, then hugged him back lightly. She wasn't an affectionate person by nature, but that was simply because she wasn't used to it. "Perhaps I was never cut out for this mother job...but I'll try and be more understanding, for you, Ugly."

"Thank you, Mom!"

The group watched as the waterfowl mother and son waddled off, Harrey wiping at something in his eye. Madnes looked sidelong at him. "What? It's eye sweat," he insisted.

"Well, I'm glad that's settled." Cheshire propped his paws on hips. "Even if rather rash words were used." He glanced up at Madnes pointedly.

"It had to be done. That's what the Madness Solver job is, right? Resolving conflicts." Madnes flashed a smile.

Cheshire just shook his head, speechless.

"The Runaway Ugly Duckling case is solved." Madnes made a check motion in the air, checking it off. "Now, let me revel in this moment of peace before it fast fades away."

"Aren't you gonna investigate that Syn stuff and Oz?" Harrey interrupted, and Madnes let his head fall backwards, staring blankly up at the sky.

"Yes…the moment of peace fast fades away."

❈26❈

ᴸᴜʀᴋɪɴɢ ᴘᴏʀᴛᴀʟ

ᴘʀᴏʙʟᴇᴍ

Beep! Beep!
Cheshire eyed the screen. Within the secret investigation room in his cottage, equipment there monitored both worlds and the linking portals. The sensors were picking up multiple signals now and beeping.

"The portals are quite active today. But why?" His cat eyes narrowed.

Pockets of space were forming across Wonderland—a great number of them.

He traced their destination, and they seemed to be connecting themselves to Oswick. It was normal for one or two pockets to form and then vanish, as Wonderland and Earth were closely linked by the portals. But this amount was off the scale! Only an interfering outside force could cause something so strange.

"This isn't good... I need to investigate further, before things get out of hand." He dashed for the door, shrugging on an overcoat and small hat. "I'd better get a message over to Madnes."

A knife *thunked* into a tree, off to the side from a nailed-up target.

Cosmic Hunter shook his shaggy head, watching his nephew's sad progress at knife-throwing.

"No, no, boy. Ya can't hold it like that. Thing's not a carrot. Hold the blade end flat between your fingers."

"How am I supposed to know?" Madnes threw again, and missed.

A bird squawked angrily at him.

"Usin' the power's force is what saps your life away, which is why you need t' strengthen your body. But I don't think it helpin' you memorize and learn stuff saps any. Rose was always learnin' new stuff, and I'm sure that's not what did her in."

"What did, *um*, do her in?"

"Never found out, t' be honest. I suspect it was somethin'

to do with Wonderland—some crisis that made her use up too much power," said Cosmic. "All right, you watch me with that there power hidden inside yer noggin', and let it memorize what I do."

The knife flew from Uncle's hand, spinning gracefully until the tip met with the target bullseye. He straightened in satisfaction, hands on belted hips. "Now, you let the power copy those motions," he told him. "Let the power guide you, but don't use it."

"Guide, but don't use." Madnes stretched his arms, flexed his hands, and wiggled his fingers dramatically, as if summoning some mysterious force to awaken. He breathed in deeply. Then his eyes shot open. His arm drew back and he threw.

The blade veered off course, almost hitting a dog who lay watching; it yelped and dodged to the side.

"Whoops!" Madnes ran over to the mutt. "Ah, maybe you should move, Muttle, and not be so close to the target."

The dog stared accusingly up at him through large, glaring eyes.

"Not be so close to the whole yard, either." Cosmic smirked. Madnes glared his way. "You aren't awakenin' that power like you ought to, boy. What's the matter? It has to be awake t' guide you."

"How should I know?" Madnes shot back. Was there any point to this training? Uncle believed that if he could defend himself, then the fairy power wouldn't have to take over and protect him during rough situations. But would it really lengthen his lifespan all that much?

"Hmm." Cosmic stroked his stubble chin, and surmised, "There's too much clutterin' up yer mind—that's what's goin' on here. Ya can't train when your brain is off flyin' in the clouds."

He grabbed Madnes by the shoulders and steered him out the backyard gate. "I can't have you killin' my dog over a missin' brain. Go out there n' find it—don't come back until you do."

"But Mom grounded me for not coming home that night—" Madnes protested.

"I'll deal with that. Now, off ya go!"

Cast out of the yard, Madness trudged glumly down the street beyond the house, heading towards downtown.

For a moment, he considered going over to Alice's. He needed to talk with her.

He knew where his mind was: it was off thinking about her and worried if she was avoiding him on purpose. He hadn't caught sight of her since the day they'd returned from Wonderland.

Madness felt a presence suddenly lurking behind him, and a finger tapped his shoulder.

Madnes spun around, hands raised in a karate chop, and came face to face with a beaming grin. He lurched backwards. "Harrey, what the heck! Why do you have to freak me out like that?"

Harrey put on a mock hurt face. "My smile should make you happy. Your words have stabbed me through the heart!"

"Oh shut up."

Harrey chuckled. "By the way! I've been seeing all sorts of strange things since after Wonderland. Weird critters running around—like those." Madnes followed his point to a line of bananas lurking and waddling around a row of parked steam cars. "Walking bananas, and they've got weird little faces with ninja headbands."

Madnes's eyebrows lowered. "Ninja bananas. Yeah, don't get too close to those. They're evil. I know from experience."

Harrey gave him an odd look. Then his face suddenly

brightened, and he shielded his eyes with a hand from the sun's hazy light. "Hey, it's Alice! Wanna join us in being lazy bums today, Alice?" he hollered, waving his other hand.

'*Alice?*' Madnes turned in the direction Harrey waved and caught sight of short blonde hair disappearing behind the patch of trees beside a rundown building. Without a second thought, he dashed over to the spot.

He had to talk to her—now or never!

Entering the trees, his boots skidded across the dirt, and he called her name. Nothing but a few robins were there to hear him, though, their heads cocked sideways.

He turned about. "Alice...please, I just want to talk," he implored to the silent tree trunks and dappled light. "This isn't like you. You're the one who's always been there—the one who I could always talk to."

He let his forehead rest against a tree and ran his fingers down the prickly bark. "Don't tell me I've lost you...?"

A robin chirped and flapped away.

"Youuu!"

Madnes lifted his head at the call, and would have hoped it was Alice, if he hadn't recognized the voice. He tensed and readied to run.

"I thought you had died—*all* of you!" Inspector Coolette approached, the last person he wanted to see right now.

The man marched toward him, single eye glaring fiercely. His appearance was unusually unkempt, as if he'd been in distress. "Nothing was left of you youngsters. I searched *everywhere*! The Sacred Pond's entire facility had to be shut down while I searched! Where did you go? How were you not vaporized?"

"Ah, Inspector." Madnes backed up, putting on a polite smile and looking for a way to escape. "We flew out. The flying bicycle, remember?"

Coolette paused and gave that a thought.

"Oh, were you worried about us? Is that why you look so…unkempt?"

Coolette's cheeks colored. "W-worried?" He turned aside and cleared his throat. "I could charge you for unauthorized entry into the Sacred Pond, boy—the punishment of which can be *extremely* severe!" The wings on his eyepatch fluttered angrily. "However, since I am a lenient and fair person, I won't do so. You are young. *Hmph*, but you must still suffer arrest and punishment for other charges."

By now Harrey had caught up and stood behind Madnes's shoulder. "Arrest?" he exclaimed.

Madnes grumbled under his breath. He didn't want to do what he was about to do—*he really didn't*—but desperate times called for desperate measures…

"Us? B-but we're just teenagers." Madnes donned a shy, innocent expression, cupping his hands together before him. "How could we have known it was illegal to fly over the compound?"

Harrey watched, in shock.

Coolette shifted uncomfortably. "Flying isn't technically illegal…"

Yes, Madnes had him now. "It was just a little prank, a joke—we're young, you know. But I didn't mean for it to go so far." He let his violet eyes plead up at the man like an innocent doe.

Back a ways, Harrey seemed both impressed and repulsed.

Coolette's face twitched, struggling not to cave in under that pleading, hopeful gaze—a gaze that Madnes had learned to master as a child to manipulate adults.

"That's—it's—*erm*—" Coolette drew back. "I—I suppose I could, *erm*, just let you off with a warning…"

"Would you?" Madnes beamed like a happy lamb, and Coolette took a farther step back.

"I'll still be watching you, though! Don't you forget that, Hatter boy." The inspector pointed, finger almost touching the tip of his nose. He turned on his heel then, stumbled, and marched out of the grove. "*Always* watching."

Madnes winked and gave a salute, then faced Harrey wearily. "And I hope I never have to humiliate myself like that ever again, as long as I live."

"Agreed. That was brutal." Harrey made a show of rubbing his eyes, as if his eyeballs had been seared by the shocking image. "Say, wasn't Alice just here?"

Madnes glanced to the side and tucked his hands in his pants pockets, moving past Harrey and returning to the street.

Harrey followed with a shrug.

Munch, krunch.

"Hey, there's some weirdo on the sidewalk," said Harrey. "Dude, those clothes look awful on him."

"Ignore him. I've had enough of weirdoes for the past few days."

But Harrey continued to stare. "There's something familiar about his face, too."

"What?" Madnes craned his neck. The *weirdo* munched lazily at a head of lettuce in one hand and stared dreamily up at nothing; a breeze whisked his thick purple mop of hair.

"Pelur, *here*? Oh no." Madnes let his footsteps drag him towards the knight, who was dressed in tattered pants, a thick belt and leather vest.

Pelur's face brightened, coming back to reality at the sight of his highly esteemed comrade. "Sir Madnes!"

"What went wrong this time? And please don't tell me it's another waterfowl causing trouble..."

Pelur cocked his head. "No," he drawled. "I'd say it's more cat than waterfowl." Madnes raised an eyebrow. "There are problems with the portals. Cheshire wants you to wait here and keep an eye peeled on things, and also to work on any cases that pop up."

Madnes resisted the urge to chew his nail and instead pressed his thumb to his lip in thought, ignoring the *crunch munch* of lettuce.

"Alone on my own again, huh? Why do I feel like this is a bad sign..."

✵27✵
ℌHE ℭURSED
ℱOREST

Rain pattered the streets, and three small figures huddled under a large cardboard box, taking shelter from the wet and cold.

"Where are we going to live now?" a young boy asked, auburn hair plastered damp around his face.

"Anywhere is better than that orphanage." The young brunette glowered out at the rain, her lips pressed thin. "I'm tired of being bullied and worked like a slave."

Someone's stomach growled.

The third kid shook his head of ash-gray curls. "We'll find a place, Nico, Drisel. Don't worry," he tried to reassure them.

"Don't worry? Ever since we ran away last week, we've had nothing but boxes and culverts to live in." Nico frowned at him, and then at the rain. "You talk as if a home is so easy to come by," he growled under his breath.

Ash didn't reply.

"I'm cold…" The girl rubbed at her bare arms, as if doing so long enough might drive the cool moisture out of the air. Ash curled an arm around her shoulders—body heat was the only source of warmth he could offer.

"We'll find a place, Drisel," he told her, and she closed her tired eyes. "God won't abandon us; we just gotta keep searching."

Nico shifted and turned away from them, anger and hurt burning inside his chest until a weary sleep engulfed him.

Kaw, kaw!

Nico jolted awake at the crow's cry.

The rain had stopped, and early dawn made scattered puddles glow like eerie mirrors beyond their box shelter. He shifted, and saw his companions were still sleeping. Without a sound, he crept out into the cool early air still heavy with moisture. He hugged his arms around himself, his sleeves worn thin.

E.E. RAWLS

A crow cawed from its perch on a chimney of one of the houses lining the alley. The black bird stared down at him, its eyes strangely gray.

"Home!" said the crow, before it flapped and flew from the alley.

Did that bird just *speak*?

On an impulse Nico ran after it, following as the crow glided past streets and away from the edge of town, over a path cut through woods and farmland. The path opened onto a bare field, and there, at the edge, rose a forest.

Nico halted. This place was different from other forests, though he couldn't say how just by looking at it—more of a feeling in the air and a scent on the breeze. Mist curled around the dark edges; trees and foliage rose thickly like a barrier.

He stood at a distance, watching.

Kaw! With a flash of black feathers, a young man appeared off to his left, wrapped in a black frock coat. "Home," spoke the mysterious older boy. "That is what you are looking for, yes?"

Nico nodded, dumbfounded.

"I know of a place, a wonderful place, filled with all the things you could ever want in life. And any person—no matter who they are—is welcome. Even orphans such as you."

"Where? What place?" Nico asked, entranced by the promise.

The older teen leaned forward, stray blond strands falling into his thick eyelashes. "Wonderland," he answered. "But there's only one way to get there."

A hand took Nico's shoulder, steering him around to face the forest. "You have to go through this forest. Wonderland awaits on the other side."

Nico gazed across at the forest whose trees resembling foreboding arms rose to the sky. He couldn't be sure, but he thought he saw something glow—a white orb peering through the overgrown brush and mist, watching him, before it blinked away. The hair on the nape of his neck rose. "What's in that forest? People call it the Forest of the Haunted, don't they?"

The young man shrugged. "Same things that are in any forest, I should think," he said. "It's a short walk before it connects to Wonderland."

Nico's gaze cut sideways up at him. "How do I know Wonderland is a real place?"

With a flourish, black wings unfolded from the teenager's back through slits in the coat. "Because that's where I live— it's *my* home. The place where people like us belong. There is no curse, only adult superstitions."

Nico looked from him and the startling pair of wings back to the forest. A place to belong—a home; they could finally have one.

No more searching, no more sleeping in the rain and dark of night. God was taking too long to help them, so he would do it himself.

"Will you lead me there?" he asked the crow person.

A smile tilted Oz's lips, but it did not reach the cold light of his eyes. "Of course."

Drisel found a scrap of paper next to her when her palm crunched down on it by accident. Curious, she smoothed the paper out to read the few written words. And then her face went still in fear.

"What?" Ash noticed and reached for the paper. She stared blankly at nothing while he read, and she heard the paper crumple in his fist. "How could he be so stupid...?" he said, almost a whisper. "I'm going after him."

Drisel jolted. "No! No, you can't go there!" She chased after Ash out of the brick alley, splashing through rain puddles.

"I can't leave him alone out there," Ash shouted back, his bare feet taking the path out of town. "Curse or no curse, he's like family and I'm going after him!"

"You'll die!" she shrieked behind him. "Nobody who goes inside that forest comes back—they vanish forever! The forest is evil."

Raindrops beaded on her eyelashes as she ran after him, the overcast sky swirling overhead like an angry sea. She hurried across the field they came to. The Forest of the Haunted loomed ahead, swathed in mist churned by the light rain. "There are things in there—undead things. The cursed ones of the forest."

Ash stopped at the very edge, his head tipped back, taking in the sight of the forest so thick it could have been a jungle from another world.

"Aren't you worried about Nico?" he asked her.

She halted a pace behind him and clasped her hands together. "Yes, of course! But if it's too late, and you get trapped in there..."

"I'm the only one who can help him. Nobody else cares about us, Drisel."

At that she was silent, though her mouth worked, searching for words.

"I'll be back with him." Ash sprinted forward without hesitation, crossing the boundary of mist, into the undergrowth.

To her it seemed as if the branches and leaves drew back, allowing him through before stretching out and blocking him from her sight like a curtain of green drawn closed.

"No..." Her breath quickened, and she shrieked at the pelting rain. "Ash!"

Only a peel of thunder answered her desperate cry.

❋28❋

INTO THE

DARKNESS

Her bare feet scratched against the pavement as Drisel ran, dodging puddles from the new wave of pelting rain. She was focused on only one thing: finding help.

But Ash was right, nobody cared—not for a pack of orphans who'd run away from the place all orphans were supposed to be kept. What they didn't know was how awful a place the orphanage was—how most orphanages really were on the inside, full of bullies and managed by indifferent adults.

Guilt nagged at her for not having helped Nico more. Maybe if she and Ash had given him more attention and support, he wouldn't have run off like a hero determined to solve all their problems by himself, determined to find them a place to belong. Now he was gone, and Ash gone after him, into the Forest of the Haunted.

Why go there, of all places? How did he get such a foolish idea in his head?

Her ragged breath put out puffs of mist into the damp air. She had no idea where she was going, just that she had to find help. Not the police—they would drag her back to the orphanage and consider her friends unsolved missing cases.

The empty soaked streets seemed to laugh at her. No one was here. No one would help. She should just give up.

Exhaustion brought her to her knees. Soaked brunette bangs blurred her vision. Drisel tipped her head back, letting the rain wash her tears and drown her sobs.

A curious glass door stood to her right, with a sign above it reading: *Madness Solver: we solve cases, not shenanigans.*

Madnes swallowed down the last coffee drops in his mug. He was about to suggest that Harrey and Knight Pelur find something else better to do than munching lettuce and building gadgets in his office space, when the door suddenly jingled open.

In from the rain came a pile of rags and matted brown hair. Madnes had to blink twice before he registered it was a human child.

"Help! You have to help them!" The girl stumbled forward and collapsed on the floor.

"What the—?" Harrey started, but Madnes was already at her side and sitting her upright.

"Harrey, bring that towel over here."

A small hand gripped the front of Madnes's shirt. "Sign says you solve c-cases, don't you?" the girl asked. "You help p-people, don't you?" she said again, more desperate.

He nodded. "Anything that's feasible, yes." He wrapped the handed towel around her frail shoulders and head, working to soak up the rainwater before she caught cold. "Where are your parents? A kid shouldn't be out on the streets alone, especially in weather like this."

But she pushed the towel away and faced him, her features weak yet determined. "Th-there's no time to worry over me. You have to help *them!*" she insisted.

Harrey knelt on the opposite side of her; he usually worked well with kids. "Calm down, now, little miss. We'll help whoever it is. But you've gotta take it easy, first."

"You don't understand!" Her shout rang in their ears. "They're dying! Help them now, or it'll be too late!"

"Too late?" Harrey shared an alarmed look with him.

Madnes kept outwardly calm. He held the girl by the shoulders, peering into her young eyes. "Tell me: who, what, and where?"

She didn't hesitate. "Nico and Ash, my family. Nico ran into the Forest of the Haunted—something about looking for a home in Wonderland, whatever that is. And then Ash...he ran after him."

Her eyes were pools of dread.

Pelur made a sound, a low grumble, and Madnes looked up from her to him. "What? Do you know the place?"

Pelur's brow creased. "The Forest of the Haunted is one of several places in Oswick that is closely attached to Wonderland. That forest is linked to a very dangerous forest in Wonderland of the same name—a place Wonderlanders avoid at all costs." Pelur's sharp, elegant features turned grim. "Pockets of linked space open and close erratically there. If one happens to be open while you venture through that particular forest in Oswick, you will find yourself walking into Wonderland's Forest of the Haunted...and you will be lost and consumed by it."

Shrugging on his maroon jacket and top hat, Madnes followed Pelur's lead into the rain. Thankfully, it was lessening. The little girl, Drisel, kept ahead of them, determined to see her friends rescued; Harrey tried to keep hold of her hand.

When they reached an open field, and Pelur came to a halt, Madnes saw it: a looming forest at the edge of the grass, mist curling around its shadowed borders. Even from a distance he could feel a prickling energy in the air that made the hairs along his skin rise.

"It's like a living thing, that forest." Pelur observed the trees, thick as jungle. "If there were ever a reason to believe Syn exists, it is that forest. It's evil. It hungers..." he growled. "Hungers for more souls to make into its children. The Haunted Ones: they are the cursed children of the forest, those who wandered in and never came out. They can never leave its grasp, neither living nor dead, forever a part of the forest."

Madnes swallowed, fear caught in his throat. He was about to step forward when Pelur's gauntleted hand grabbed his shoulder. "A person who enters has only 24 hours to live before the forest takes them."

"Takes them…what do you mean?"

"After 24 hours, you will become a Haunted One—forever bound to the forest's will. That is the curse people speak of."

The old Madnes would have guffawed and dismissed it all as fantasy, but he knew better now—you don't just dismiss things.

"But when did Nico enter the forest? That gives us far less than 24 hours to save him. Not that it isn't doable, right?"

Pelur shook his damp head. "It's like a labyrinth in there. Once you go in, things change and shift. The forest will do whatever it can to make you lost and keep you within it."

"…Great. That's just great." Madnes fidgeted with his boots. "Tell me, is there *anything* in Wonderland that's pleasant and happy?"

Pelur cocked his head sideways, not getting the sarcasm.

"Beware nightfall, Sir Madnes—that's when the poor souls of those who've already been taken awake. They roam the forest in search of lost people…to turn them. You must beware of both time and *them*, Sir."

Madnes patted his top hat more securely on his head. "Keeps getting better and better, doesn't it? Okay." He sucked in a deep breath. "I'm off! Before I lose all courage."

"Wait! Use this." Harrey placed a compass-like gadget in his palm. "Whatever that wicked forest tries, you use this to find your way back out."

Madnes hefted it in his palm. "Thanks." He smiled past his nerves and buttoned the compass into a pocket. They had all wanted to come with him, but he refused, insisting a group would be more cumbersome and difficult to keep track of.

Much as he didn't want to go alone, he refused to put more lives at risk. Besides, he had the Madness Solver power.

"Twenty hours; I'll be back by then!" Madnes waved and trotted toward the forest.

He stepped through the wall of curling mist and approached the trees. Leaves and branches furled aside for him. He ventured through the foliage.

"I'm going with you!" Drisel appeared, and before he could protest, she dove in after him.

✸29✸

FOREST OF THE

HAUNTED

A crow circled the treetops once before flapping away. "You will fail this time, Madnes," Oz cawed to the air. "And it will finally break you…"

"Drisel!" Madnes grabbed for the little girl's arm. Heavy foliage moved to obscure the spot where they'd entered the forest.

"Let go!" Drisel tried to yank free. "I'm coming with you— I won't go back!"

He knew how she felt, but the child would be in too much danger here, not to mention be a distraction for him.

He shoved low branches and veils of vines aside, moving to take her back out of the forest. More greenery lay beyond what he'd just pushed aside. He sucked in a breath and pushed forward, shoving more leaves away. More and more and more.

Where was the field? Why was the way out not showing itself?

Madnes swallowed down a surge of panic. No matter how much he dug at the foliage, there was nothing but more leaves beyond his hands.

Pelur's words came to mind: *"It's like a labyrinth in there. Once you go in, things change and shift. The forest will do whatever it can to make you lost and keep you within it."*

Madnes released the foliage, letting it swing back in place, and he backed up until he was beside Drisel on a narrow winding path. "We can't get out the same way we came in, huh?" His voice sounded small and muffled in the thick atmosphere.

Drisel blinked up at him. He had to keep his cool; she was counting on him, now. "Promise you'll do as I say and won't let go of my hand?" he told her, taking her hand in his.

She tipped her face up at the green ceiling, and he took a moment to do the same.

Faint light filtered down through a soupy, green canopy, mist spilling around it like small streams.

"Okay," he heard her agree.

Hand in hand, their shoes squished dirt and rotting leaves as they followed the path that was more like a deer-run.

The forest held an eerie glow from the rainy day's filtered light above, yet not a drop of water touched their heads. A musty scent permeated the air: rich soil and moss, filling his nose. And there were no sounds but their footsteps through a graveyard-like stillness.

Flap, flap!

Madnes's heart jumped, and he yanked the girl's hand to a halt.

"It's a bird," Drisel spoke up reassuringly. He looked to where she pointed at a blue jay. Something about the bird's beak unnerved him, as if it were smiling grimly at them.

He tugged her onward, eager to leave it behind.

Large flowers opened as they passed by, some as tall as he was. A bubbling liquid spilled down their petals, and he was careful to steer clear.

Yellow fruits hung down from tendrils of moss, some across their path, forcing them to duck under to get around them.

The fruits put out a pungent scent. Drisel's stomach growled, but he refused to let her taste one.

After a while, it felt like they had been walking for *hours* — or was it just a few minutes? Time felt like a distorted thing here. He checked his pocket watch: 18 hours left.

He had to pick up the pace. But to where? Where was he going? How do you find someone who's lost in a forest?

He racked his Madness Solver brain for ideas. Prints in the dirt, snapped twigs, places to hide...his eyes scanned, but he hadn't come across any footprints or decent places to shelter.

There were a few snapped twigs, but that could be from anything.

The best option—and also the worst—was to make as much noise as possible and call out their names. He really didn't like that idea. But it was the fastest approach—and fast was what they needed.

"Hey, Drisel." He told the little girl his plan, and her already wide gaze widened further.

"You want the Haunted Ones to find us? Are you mad?" she said.

"It's still daytime, even if a bit gloomy from the rainclouds. The Haunted don't come out until nightfall, remember? According to Knight Pelur, anyway."

"What if *other* things live here?"

Madnes shifted uncomfortably, craning his neck and eyeing the trees heavy with moss to either side of the path. "It's our only hope of finding your friends in time."

And so, that was what they did.

"Aaash!"

"Nicooo!"

Their calls rang out, but the dense atmosphere wouldn't let their voices carry far.

Was it just him, or did the vines move closer? He checked his watch again: 17 hours left.

Something broke free from a wall of bushes off to his left. A high pitch growl split the silence, hurting his ears, and a tangle of creature limbs came charging out at them.

It moved like a blur. Madnes had time only to grab Drisel up and duck around a tree trunk. Claws scratched up the soil as it missed them.

Madnes lunged over a fallen tree and zigzagged through the forest's tangle of trunks, roots and undergrowth, his free arm knocking aside low branches, his head ducking under what he could. It was like weaving through a thick maze. And as fast as his feet carried him, the creature could still be heard somewhere not far behind.

Drisel clutched her arms around his neck as he held her, staring wildly over his shoulder.

"What *is* that thing?" he barely spared a breath to ask her over the commotion of the chase. Her alarmed expression was silent.

Maybe the creature moved too fast for any features to be identified.

Madnes let the power carry his legs across the forest floor in wide strides. More high pitch growls drew near—more of the many-limbed creatures had joined in the hunt.

Drisel whimpered in his ear.

Madnes made a dodge around a large boulder that rose suddenly from the undergrowth and found his footsteps running across stone. A bird twittered above, and he realized the forest had suddenly fallen silent behind him.

He slid to a stop and turned. The creatures were nowhere to be seen.

Drisel wriggled free and plopped to the ground. An old structure had once been here, now nothing but ruins, a stone platform and broken pillars.

"There's a face in the tree," she said.

Madnes moved to her side, stepping around thick roots which wove through and broke up a portion of the platform. Protruding from the left side of the tree she pointed to, was something like cheeks, a nose, and what could be closed eyes. Something almost human, yet of bark.

A chill crawled up his skin, and he pulled Drisel away from the face before she could reach and poke a finger at it. "It's like a person. Is a person stuck inside the tree?"

"...I don't know," he whispered.

The Haunted Ones…the cursed children of the forest…neither living nor dead, forever a part of the forest…

"Look, Mr. Madnes, there's another one."

This face had half a torso attached, its arms clinging to a tree as if in sleep, all smooth bark surface, hair and eyelashes a tangle of moss.

Madnes gripped Drisel's hand. What light filtered down from the canopy was fading fast.

Was it a trick of shadow, or did one of those closed eyes in the bark move?

❁30❁
The Haunted
Ones

Madnes tugged on Drisel's hand, hurrying to get as far away as possible from the grove of trees and human faces sunk in bark. Daylight had fallen fast—faster than he had anticipated.

At nightfall, the Haunted Ones roam the forest in search of those who don't belong.

He had to find Ash and Nico before *they* found them. "And before *they* find us," he murmured.

The mist, hovering in the forest canopy during the day, now descended, its tendrils wrapping around roots and forest growth. He couldn't see his boots. It was like wading through swamp water.

Damp air stirred around him as if the forest had let out a breath. Tree limbs cracked and wood groaned. Something rumbled briefly along the ground.

Drisel grabbed at his hand with both of hers, and her head turned every which way in the darkness. He could barely make out her features, the light vanished so swiftly.

"Mr. Madnes," she spoke in a whisper. "The forest is waking up."

A deep, throaty rumble passed through the surrounding trees before all went eerily silent.

"The children of the forest…they'll find us."

Madnes urged her to keep moving, his hand in hers a comfort. "You leave the worrying to me. For now, just focus on finding your friends."

As soon as the words left his lips, a shadow moved swiftly from behind one tree to another, darker than night. He stared at the spot not far away. "Keep moving, Drisel."

The mist took on a faint blue glow with the onset of deep night. Much as it unnerved him, the faint glow was a source of light that they needed, however dim it was. He hurried the girl onward, weaving around gray shapes of moss-buried trunks and reaching vines.

"Ash! Nico!" He called out as low as he could without actually shouting. It felt like his voice wasn't carrying at all, the thick air grasped and extinguished the words.

A second shadow dashed across his vision. He whipped around to face it. Wood groaned and creaked in the night.

A tree limb suddenly reached for his back.

Madnes let go of Drisel and fell sideways, and the bark hand missed. He rolled back up to his feet.

A shadow in the shape of a human glided toward Drisel, a pair of eyes glowing void of life. A Haunted One.

She screamed, and Madnes yanked her by the wrist, pulling her away. He scooped her up in his arms, putting his power-charged legs to work. He dodged, ducked, and bounded—weaving his way in the opposite direction of the following shadows. Could he lose them somehow? The forest felt thicker, closing in around them.

Running on what was once a path, Madnes wondered if his vision was going double or if the trees now tangled closer and closer together, working to choke out the path and stop their escape.

The forest will do whatever it can to keep you...

He spared a glance over his shoulder. A shadow and glowing eyes trailed the path after them, gliding effortlessly and swiftly toward their fleeing backs. Hands encrusted in bark reached out, tangles of hair and leaves flowed back from a too-human face.

Madnes swung his head back around to speed up his pace, and came face-to-face with white, pupilless eyes.

"Ahh!"

A twig-and-skin hand swiped for them, lethally sharp.

He shifted his arms and torso, holding Drisel, pulling her out of the way but exposing his back. Twig claws sliced through his jacket. He winced.

"Your soul. We want your soul."

A second twig-hand reached, and Madnes struggled to twist around and veer off the path. But the Haunted One behind them had now caught up and drew near like a ghost. The voice, the void eyes, pulled at him like invisible ropes.

His body shuddered, his soul inside his chest weakened under their gaze.

"*Give it to us. Become one with the forest. Appease the forest. Serrrve the forest...*"

The tread of his boots pressed into the soil as he launched himself off the path.

Bark fingers clawed the air for his hair, his arms, his jacket—just missing him.

The children of the forest screeched in rage, coming after him into the vine-and-root tangled depths.

'*I won't make it—I need help!*' Madnes thought desperately.

But there was no help. No one was here to help, except for a fairy who wanted to eat away his life.

He thought back to his uncle's faith, and made a decision.

'*God, if You do hear me and really care, please—please help us! If not for my sake, then for Drisel and her friends.*'

Praying for help only when he absolutely needed it—that's what most everybody did when they were in distress. Going about life, never thinking or caring about God until something bad happened. Then they prayed, then they cared. He was like that, and a part of him felt suddenly ashamed, asking for help when he'd never cared much about the Creator before.

'*If I never cared, then why should He care?*' he thought.

5 hours left, read the clock.

His leg muscles ached, tiring out.

He would have to ask the fairy for more power than just muscle strength, and lose a portion of his life, if his body couldn't continue.

He pushed on, struggling, and dove through a rising cloud of mist that suddenly billowed up before them. He desperately hoped it could somehow hide them.

"*This way...*"

Mist churned around him everywhere, stirred by the forest's cool breath.

Groans and creaks sounded off to his left, then to his right. He held Drisel close.

Something in the mist beckoned. A small shape with flowing hair. A palm outstretched like a ghost's. *"Come,"* it said.

The voice sounded different from the others, an airy whisper.

Madnes took a chance and stumbled forward blindly after the fading image. The person vanished, and he used his free hand to feel out through the mist. His fingertips felt nothing but fog moisture at first, then a rough rock surface came across his touch, and he moved to duck down behind it, with Drisel huddled against his chest.

❄31❄

CHILD OF THE
FOREST

Shapes moved through the billowing mist. Eyes like lanterns of the Haunted Ones came and went. Time ticked by like a steady rain, and Madnes feared to move and risk detection.

His head started to feel stuffy, and his eyelids drooped down several times.

He shook himself, trying to stay awake.

1 hour left.

No, no, there wasn't time! Even if he found the orphan children, they'd still have to find their way out of the forest's maze. One hour wasn't enough—he had to find those kids *now*!

A faint beam of light drew softly through the mist.

It was followed by another, the faint light of dawn, he realized, and it broke through the canopy and gave the air a golden glow.

No more shapes moved about. The Haunted Ones were returning to their slumber. The thick fog retreated slowly back up into the shadowed niches of the trees, where it would wait until nightfall once more.

Madnes carefully stood and pulled a sleepy Drisel with him.

His boots sunk into wet soil, and he looked down to see they'd been hiding behind a boulder at the edge of a small pool, its water murky and layered with algae. A large tree overgrown with rich green mosses grew from the pool's depths at a slant. An odd shape had perched on the lowest limb—and as sunlight chased shadows away, and dust mots glimmered in the air, Madnes watched the shape move and climb down.

Dappled light played across auburn hair, and a set of fair eyes locked onto him. The young kid hopped onto dry land and moved across the forest floor with ease on his bare feet. His tattered clothes rippled as if stirred by an unfelt breeze.

Drisel saw him and immediately wrenched herself free from Madnes. "Nico!" she cried and barreled into him.

He stumbled, and a faint smile touched his face. But there was a distant look in his eyes, a part that the smile wasn't reaching. It made Madnes uneasy.

"Drisel..." Nico's voice rustled like leaves in the wind. "You should not have risked your life to find us."

"How can you say that?" Drisel held him by the arms, tears bubbling.

But Nico's gaze dropped down and away from her.

Madnes waited, studying the boy up and down. Tendrils of vines tangled throughout Nico's hair, and velvety moss crawled up the sides of his face and the fronts of his arms and feet.

He was already a part of the forest.

"Nico?" Drisel asked again, concern marring her features. "What happened to you?"

Madnes stepped forward and placed a hand on her frail shoulder. "Is it too late?" Madnes knew he didn't want to hear the answer the moment he asked. He *was* too late; of course he was. They never knew the exact time that Nico had entered the forest. They only had a rough guess based on when the other orphan, Ash, went in after him.

'I failed... Darn it all, I failed!'

A fine thread held his emotions back, keeping the scream inside him leashed.

Nico met his gaze, then turned his face to the side with a sad look that contradicted the peaceful smile on his lips. "It's not too late for *him*." He nodded up at the mossy tree.

Propped up on intersecting branches was another boy, flecks glinting on the curls of his ash hair. He slept balled up in rags.

Nico stretched out his hand, and a limb from the tree wrapped around and lifted Ash, placing him carefully down beside Drisel. Ash's eyelids fluttered halfway open.

"Drisel... Drisel?" Ash murmured, his eyes half glazed over. He was barely conscious, and specks of green speckled the flesh of his cheeks.

"He doesn't have long," said Nico. "You must take him out of the forest. I will help guide you, while I still have control over myself."

Madnes nodded and scooped Ash's limp form up in his arms.

The noise of scurrying limbs and angry growls sounded behind the trees as Madnes and Drisel hurried after Nico, who held Harrey's compass and led them through the maze of green. Trees appeared to shift and gather like a wall to block their path, and Nico swiftly navigated them around—dodging roots that rose to snatch their feet.

The forest was fighting to keep them in.

Krrsh! A pack of blurry creatures with many limbs burst out of the underbrush near Madnes's right—the creatures from before. He tried to lift Drisel while still carrying Ash, but the blurs were moving fast. He placed himself between them and the children, and shielded with his body, bracing for impact.

Nico thrust his palms out, fingers splayed, eyes flashing a vibrant green.

Wood crunched and ripped, and vines like whips dropped down and flung at the creatures—tangling them up like spider webs.

"Hurry!"

The foliage weaved thicker. Madnes and Drisel shoved their way through, knocking and pushing ferns and thorny bushes aside, climbing over roots that reached to drag them under the soil.

Following behind, Nico focused, trying to force the foliage back. "The forest is fighting my influence...she doesn't want to let you go. You must hurry! I can barely hold it back..."

"Drisel, hold my arm!" Madnes told her. She didn't hesitate.

With both orphans in tow, he charged forward.

KRrsh, krnch! Wood broke and vines snapped as he tore forward, a trickle of power bolstering his muscles. Welts across his arms and back stung, but he plowed ahead, forcing a way out whether the forest willed it or not, and losing his hat to the clawing branches in the process.

One final crack of a shoved-aside bush, and bright daylight beat down on them from a blue sky.

His boots crunched upon the soil of an overgrown field.

They were out!

Drisel gave a joyful shout, and Madnes set Ash down as he released the power and a wave of weariness flooded through his body.

The girl turned back around and paused at the forest's foggy edge behind them. "Nico?" she called and held out her hand. "You're coming too, right?"

Nico met her hopeful gaze with regret. "This was all my fault, Drisel. I'm so sorry... Ash, I'm so sorry."

She kept her hand out, until he finally explained, "It's too late for me, Drisel."

"No!" Drisel's voice choked. She tried to grab his hand, but he pulled back, deeper into the leaves.

Ash sat up and stared after their friend, slowly regaining consciousness. Emotions wrote across his face the words that his mouth couldn't yet say.

Nico's gaze moistened. "I should've known better. We were warned about this forest, but I didn't listen. I wanted to find us a home, so badly... I didn't want to wait for God to provide, so I listened to a stranger instead."

Tears rolled down Drisel's trembling chin. Ash shakily got to his feet.

Nico reached out to lightly touch her cheek and Ash's chest. "Don't be sad. Maybe I'll still be me, in a way, though I can never leave this place. I...will miss my other life with you."

"And we'll miss you," Ash finally spoke.

It was a heart wrenching goodbye. Drisel and Ash finally left to walk across the field toward where Harrey and Knight Pelur stood waiting for them, hand in hand and glancing back more than once.

Madnes brushed tears from his cheeks and was about to follow.

"Madness Solver."

He halted and turned back.

"Don't blame someone else for the choices I made." Nico's gaze held him. "This wasn't your fault, nor the Creator's. I was warned, but I didn't listen."

Madnes was tempted to look away. He did feel like it was his fault. If he had been stronger, better at using the power, more clever, fearless, and...and...

A light hand touched his chest. Green tendrils stirred from an unfelt breeze along Nico's arm.

"Don't despair just because I couldn't be saved, Madness Solver. Oswick still needs you." A vine carried his top hat over and Nico brushed it off. "You dropped this."

The familiar hat plopped down on Madnes's head.

"How do you know about the Madness Solver?" asked Madnes.

"The forest told me. It's a part of Wonderland." Nico's green gaze intensified. "Do this for me, will you? Save our world. Don't let anyone else become like me."

Madnes held the boy's hand in his for one brief moment, one last goodbye. "I will…I promise."

Nico's smile was almost serene as Madnes left, looking back over a shoulder one last time.

"Tell me, who was the stranger that talked you into coming here?"

"He was like a crow, and yet human," recalled the orphan. "He had blond hair and a smooth voice that tempted me to believe anything he said."

Anger flared inside Madnes's chest, and it felt like the air itself crackled.

"Oz."

❄32❄
A Very Unmerry
Day

Resting snug inside the Madness Solver office, Ash's health steadily improved, the color returning to his cheeks. The group discussed where the orphans should stay now, since Madnes didn't feel right about sending them back to the orphanage—a place they'd sacrificed so much to escape from.

"There's plenty of room at my uncle's place," suggested Harrey. "It's where I live, and I don't think he'd mind having more pairs of hands to help out around the workshop."

"It's a workshop, Harrey. Not exactly kid friendly." Madnes frowned.

Harrey waved that aside. "I was younger than these squirts when I first started tinkering in the shop! Besides, they look like clever kiddos." He patted the orphans' heads. Drisel smoothed her hair back down.

Madnes hesitated, but there really wasn't any other place they could stay. Harrey's workshop-house had plenty of room, and he was good with kids. *'Probably because he's just like one,'* he thought. "Fine. But I'm holding *you* responsible if anything happens."

Harrey waved his palms, "Okay, okay! Don't get your knickers in a twist, dude."

Madnes rolled his eyes and headed for the door.

"Where're you off to?" Harrey called after.

"Out," he replied tersely, "I need to clear my head."

Madnes walked without a destination, letting his feet take him wherever they willed. The day was too pretty for what had just happened that night, for the young life that had been lost.

Rain; he wished it would rain.

Nico, why couldn't he save him? Why did it have to be too late to save him?

'I'm to blame, no matter what he said. It's my fault.'

And Oz's fault. This was something that could not be forgiven. A life couldn't be brought back.

Madnes spotted a bench and sunk down onto it, letting his face fall in his hands, blocking out the merry daylight from his sight.

"Broooody~ brooooody~"

Madnes lifted his head a fraction. Someone was singing? Tiny, high voices were whining a tune.

He tilted his ear.

It was coming from under the bench.

He craned his neck down to look underneath him.

A cluster of daffodils swayed there, merry and yellow, and their petal-mouths opened and sang: "Broooody, you are so brooooody~ You've got nobooody to call your own~"

He grabbed a nearby bucket of rainwater and dowsed them.

The flowers coughed and hissed at him.

He hissed back. "Stupid daffodils. I am *not* brooding!"

They whined and hissed some more.

"Taking your anger out on flowers? Really, Madnes."

His head whipped around, and his face went wide seeing Alice there.

She approached, sunshine playing in her short blonde hair, a purple bow in it today. She wore a skort, vest, and shirt blouse, all green shades like a forest elf.

His memory of her skin glowing like liquid sunlight returned. What was she really? Was she finally going to stop hiding from him and talk?

Alice perched on the bench, much like she used to whenever he was feeling down about something, to lend a friendly ear. He'd missed that.

"You saw them making faces and laughing at me, the boogers," he replied.

"Wonderland flowers don't have any manners," she said. "Everybody knows that."

"*Hmph.*" He almost laughed, but too much had happened for him to really laugh. "Does this mean we're friends again?"

Her lips looked like a puckered tulip. "If you promise not to ask questions about me."

His chest sunk. But if that was what she wanted, then it was her life, her choice. He didn't have the right to pry.

"All right. I promise. But if you ever change your mind, and would like to talk," he faced her, "you know I'm here for you."

Was it a trick of the light or did she blush?

"And sorry about...you know." The line of his mouth winced.

"Ha!" Her eyebrows lowered slyly. "You think I'll forgive you so easily, Peeping Tom?" She patted his cheek roughly. "You owe me a year's worth of favors, and more, for that."

"Ahh, fine." He mock huffed and rubbed at his cheek. "I live to serve you, princess."

She grinned back at him. "I saw you all come back from the forest," she said next, her tone a touch careful. "And I forced the details out of Harrey."

"Ah. Harrey never could keep a secret." That was all he could think to say. His heart was raw thinking about the Haunted Forest, and the one who would not be returning from it.

"You can't do everything, Madnes," she said. "Not every person can be rescued. All you can do is try your best—and that's exactly what you did."

"But it's a life, Alice. A *life*. I can't brush that off. Nico's life is gone, and I was the only one who could have helped him."

Her hand lightly caressed over his. "Take your time and grieve, Madnes."

Something about those words loosened the tension in his shoulders. He was allowed to grieve.

"And remember to be thankful for those you *did* save. Don't forget about them." She smiled.

Twilight glowed a reddish purple beyond the bedroom window. Sitting on the edge of his bed, his back slouched, Madnes stared at nothing.

The top hat dangled from his fingers.

He envisioned Nico handing it back to him, green moss and vines taking over his small body while he smiled sadly.

The Madness Solver was needed, just as Cheshire had tried to tell him; he hadn't fully realized that until now. A heavy responsibility, with lives at stake.

That forest was the result of something tainting it—Syn tainting it. Whether Syn was a legend or not, there was some truth to be found in most myths.

What worried him was how closely that forest from Wonderland had melded itself with Oswick. It was a danger he had to put an end to.

"I won't forget you, Nico…" His grip tightened on the hat. "This time, I won't let you down."

"Madnes? Madnes! There's trouble."

An incessant knocking woke Madnes, giving him a headache. He pulled himself out of bed, grumbled, and tugged open the door to be greeted by Harrey's expressive face and grease-and-paint stained attire.

"What now? Don't tell me you put those kids in one of your crazy flying inventions! If they're hurt, so help me, I'll…" Madnes began.

"No, not that. It...you have to come see for yourself!" Harrey sprinted back down the stairs.

With a groan, Madnes got out of his panda pajamas, slipped on a new maroon jacket, and followed. Mom spotted them and shouted after him as he sprinted out the door: "You get back here! Madnes! You're still grounded, you—"

"Be back in a bit, Mom!"

He hurried out after Harrey, adjusting his hastily put-on clothes and buttons. "What trouble? This had better be worth the *trouble* I'm going to face from Mom..."

They reached the park, and both his trot and words slowed to a rattled halt.

The park looked like a scene out of Wonderland: the rocks were mushrooms the size of children, and flowers like rainbows sprouted in the trees; a flock of hammer-head birds perched on branches, and a two-headed snake hissed.

A normal sight for Madnes, and now for Harrey too, as he could see Wonderlanders on Earth. But the problem was the crowd of ordinary people who stood around the park, staring and gawking. It could only mean one very troublesome thing:

Normal people could see it now, too.

Something was wrong with the worlds.

"Oh...crud."

❈33❈

BETRAYAL

Madnes's mouth hung open, speechless, at the crowd of people—the crowd who could see Wonderland creatures in the town park. Even steam cars from the street across had squealed to a halt.

At Harrey's tap on his shoulder, Madnes looked back. His friend pointed at a line of ninja bananas hurrying out of the park, taking cover. "I don't think everything is visible, Madnes. It's just the park area, for some weird reason."

Madnes eyed the bananas now clear of the park, and indeed it didn't seem like anybody noticed them. "But how can people see the park like this, in the first place?" He backed up, tapping a foot and pressing his thumb to his lip, observing the situation.

The ground rumbled beneath their feet suddenly, and a flash of light blinded them.

Madnes blinked repeatedly, trying to see past the white spots dancing in his vision.

"It's gone!" he heard Harrey shout.

The white afterimages faded, and Madnes tried to see the park, but he couldn't spot a single tree, giant mushroom, or any Wonderland creatures.

Where was the park?

Dirt, bare ground. There was an expanse of nothing where the park had just been.

Harrey was right. The park was gone, along with everything and everyone in it.

Madnes swallowed, trying to keep calm yet fearing the worst.

"Where the heck is Cheshire when I need him?"

Cheshire tossed his hat aside and ran over to the open portal nearby the palace. It had grown twice its size since he and Madnes had last been there, and its watery surface roared and swirled with hurricane force.

This behavior was abnormal; he'd never seen a portal do this before.

"What could be the cause?" If it didn't stop soon, more pockets of space would form and connect to Oswick, and who knew what the consequences of that might be?

The cat trotted in his boots, circling the portal, inspecting it. If all the portals around Wonderland were doing this, then it meant the balance between worlds was being disrupted. Something or someone was to blame, and it had to be stopped fast.

"I must warn the Red King."

Cheshire turned in the direction of the palace.

He had taken no more than five steps when his keen cat ears heard a voice.

He quickly climbed up the nearest tree—not something he liked to do; he hated doing anything that resembled Earth cats, but a sense of urgency warned him to hide.

He watched and waited.

"Yes, they appear to be in working order." A short, rotund man with a long nose approached the portal below. He tapped its metal tree frame with a pen before writing something down on a clipboard in hand. "Nice…very nice."

Cheshire eyed the man from above. He recognized him as the advisor to the Red King.

Something didn't sit well. The short man seemed *pleased* about the portal being out of control.

When the advisor headed back towards the palace, Cheshire decided to follow and learn more. Keeping to the trees and bushes, his cat stealth came in handy.

The advisor continued his way into the palace, and Cheshire climbed the palace wall from windowsill to windowsill until he could sneak inside through an open window. He spotted the man again down a hall and followed him via the palace's air duct system.

The advisor entered the royal chambers.

Cheshire peeked between the bars of the vent inside the royal room wall. There the Red King sat, drinking tea, and the long-nosed man waited to speak.

"All is working properly, as you planned, Your Majesty," the advisor said, once the king's hand had signaled for him to speak. And he showed him the clipboard.

"Good." The Red King's gaze roved over whatever was written there. "The Terraforming process has begun, I see."

"Yes, Your Majesty." The short man grinned. "The crystal focal points for the spell are stable and holding strong. It's finally working—fantastically!"

"And the crowv woman inside is still contained?"

"Yes, yes of course, sire!"

Crowv woman? Crystal focal points? Cheshire tried to steady his heart's rapid pounding. The Red King was breaking the law of the portals and tampering with forbidden power? Madnes's suspicions about someone in Wonderland being up to no good had been true.

'Madnes—I must get back to him!'

In his haste, Cheshire rose to stand, and his head *thumped* the ceiling of the air duct.

"What was that?"

Cheshire covered his mouth with a paw and backed away from the vent bars.

But not fast enough before the advisor ripped off the cover.

"A cat?" the advisor exclaimed.

Cheshire hissed and leaped at his face before the man could react—claws swiping at his eyes and forcing him to draw back.

"Cheshire!" shouted the king, "Grab that cat!"

The moment his paws touched the floor, Cheshire bolted on all four limbs across the room for the door, all dignity thrown aside. His furry paws and boots slipped on the marble hallway outside the room, and he kicked his limbs forward and back, seeking a solid grip. He scurried down the hallway as they stormed behind him.

The advisor lunged, hands grabbing for Cheshire; he felt them skim above his fur.

Cheshire pivoted and turned down a sharp corner, narrowly escaping the hands. His claws *click-clicked* on the hard surface in a frantic, awkward run. His invisible power didn't work inside the palace, so he couldn't hide.

A figure appeared ahead. Cheshire tried to put all four paw-brakes on, but he couldn't stop his skid across the slick surface.

Oz looked down at the cat skidding toward his boots. With one hand he reached down and grabbed him up. His other hand pulled the hem of his royal cape around the cat in his arm, hiding Cheshire from view.

The advisor almost bumped into the prince in his hurry around the corner. "Oh, Prince Oz! Terribly sorry to disturb you," the rotund man blabbered. "You didn't by any chance see a…a cat running about, did you?" He craned his neck, looking this way and that, trying to see around Oz's much taller frame.

Oz barely moved his proud head. "A cat? No. But there is a dog here before me. Try looking in the mirror."

The advisor's face turned dark, but he backed away. "Better watch yourself, Your Highness," he said menacingly over a shoulder. "No one is safe in Wonderland. Not even your high self."

Oz held his head high.

Once the man had gone, Oz turned into the nearest room with Cheshire held tightly under his arm.

34

TERRAFORMING

Cheshire *mreeowed* as he was tossed to the floor of the small room. Oz closed and locked the door behind them, then turned and faced the cat.

"On the run from my father, are you, flaky cat?"

Cheshire stood upright, dusting at his waistcoat. "The better question, rude young man, is why did you save me from him? I won't do anything for you, if that's what you're expecting."

Oz sniffed. "As if I'd ask a favor from a cat," he said brusquely. "I simply don't like that advisor. I thought it'd be fun to cause him some stress and hide you away." The prince chuckled. "Though, I am curious…" He bent halfway down to the cat, a smirk on his lips. "Why *were* you on the run? Have you been a naughty kitty?" He leaned back from Cheshire's claw swipe.

"How long has this scheme of your father's been going on?" Cheshire growled, sounding more like a cat hiss. "And to think, there was a time when I thought well of him, and of you."

The prince tossed the royal cape back over his shoulder and narrowed his expression at the feline. "Scheme?" He turned his nose up. "I could care less what you think of me anymore, Cheshire. I've given up on that. But I haven't a clue what scheme you're referring to."

Cheshire's tail swished back and forth as he eyed the prince. Oz had no more reason to lie; it was clear Cheshire would never grant him the power from Madnes, not after the way Oz had treated the boy.

So, had the king been keeping his son in the dark about the portals too?

"In that case, I'll tell you what I overheard," he said decidedly. "The balance of the worlds has been disrupted; your father has betrayed our trust and broken the law of the portals. I fear everyone in Oswick is in danger…"

Oz's shoulders shrugged, nonchalant.

"Your father mentioned something about a Terraforming spell or process. Have you heard the name before?"

Oz's stare was blank.

"Anything about crystal focal points for a spell? And a crowy woman?"

A spark lit in Oz's eyes. "Crowy woman?"

He got close to the cat, his countenance suddenly dark. "Explain," Oz demanded.

"She's being contained, but I haven't a clue what for, where, or who she is. That was all I could overhear."

"Could it be...?" Oz's gaze cut sideways, to the room's empty fireplace and leftover flakes of ash. "Mother...is that where she's been?" He thumbed his chin in thought.

Cheshire watched the prince with caution. "The queen?" Last he and Wonderland heard, the queen had died of an illness. Did Oz have reason to believe otherwise?

"I must know the truth." Oz suddenly made for the door.

"Wait, prince!" Cheshire wasn't sure what was going on in the youth's head, but if Oz let on to the king that he knew about his father's plot, Oz could find himself in danger. "Even if you are his son, the king is a man to be feared. You must tread carefully. Don't put your life at risk, when this crowv woman could be anyone; it's highly unlikely that she is your mother."

The prince's stride paused. "I don't care about Oswick or Earth. Nothing matters to me but finding my mother—and nothing will stop me from doing so."

The king's anteroom doors flung open. Oz strode inside, his wings spread wide, the black feathers that circled the back of his head resembling a crown.

The king looked up from one of his many ornate chairs, dressed all in black but for the blood red robe.

"Is it true?" Oz demanded.

The king raised an eyebrow, both in question and rebuke.

"Cheshire passed through here. He says you're doing something with the portals, some sort of spell, and that a crowv woman is involved." Oz drew near, step by step, black feathers swirling around him angrily. "Is it *her*? Where have you been keeping Mother all this time?" he growled. "Tell me!" His shout echoed and the marble floor rumbled.

The king looked up from the game he'd been playing: a tier of boards and chess pieces. His opponent, a mechanical hand, awaited its turn.

One glance at Oz's show of anger, and the king's attention returned to the boards. "I suppose there's no longer a reason to keep it from you," he said smoothly, ignoring any threat Oz tried to pose. "It's called Terraforming, and it's a spell I'm using to cultivate the land on Earth. Oswick is the easiest place to start with. Soon, the island will be reformed and made into the likeness of our lovely Wonderland—creating a second Wonderland, if you will. Won't that be nice? Having another world under my rule, a new place our people can call home?" He stroked his thick, trimmed black beard.

Oz's expression didn't waver. "You know I don't care about any of that."

The king finally turned in his seat, every bit as imposing as when on the throne. "Your mother was ill, Oz. You saw for yourself how her health deteriorated. Why are you so set on believing she's still alive?"

Oz didn't let himself answer, instead his lips thinned together.

"There is a crowv woman, yes," admitted the king. "But it is not your mother. The crystal she's contained within is the only thing keeping her alive after battling the same illness that took your mother—the illness so many crowv people have perished from. She cannot leave it and live, at the moment, but we are using the spell to draw in energy from

Oswick and transfer it to help her recovery." His frown made the stonework of the room feel soft.

"You see, not only is the Terraforming spell giving us new land, but it is also transferring all that gathered energy to heal the sick." The king rose to his full height and in two strides reached Oz, planting a hard hand on his shoulder. "You and your mother's crowv people may no longer be in danger of extinction, thanks to this spell."

Mixed emotions whirled through Oz like a storm. He'd said it wasn't Mother, but a gut feeling didn't want him to believe anything the king said. Mother had to be out there, somewhere—and alive.

"The spell is helping her?"

The king tipped his head forward in a slight nod.

"Where is this crowv? I want to see her."

"In time, my son. There is work to be done. But once the spell is complete, you may."

"I don't want to wait," Oz persisted.

The king motioned with a hand, and an invisible force shoved Oz, skidding him back across the floor and tripping him over a carpet. "In time," he repeated.

Oz's hands clenched. But he relented. Father was powerful—he couldn't force him to talk.

But that was fine; now that he had a vague idea of where this crowv woman was—somewhere inside one of the spell's crystals—he could find her on his own.

He would find her, and see for himself who she was and if she held a clue to Mother's whereabouts.

From the safety of the small room, Cheshire listened in through a voice-catcher gadget hidden under Oz's shirt.

"Healing the crowv people?" He pawed his furry chin.

Creating a second Wonderland, having another world under his rule—how wicked! The king was willing to destroy their neighbor, Earth, just to satisfy his own greed.

"I must get to Madnes. We must find and destroy those crystals before it's too late!"

❖35❖

VANISHED

"*B*eware..." the rocking-horse dragonfly had rasped in Madnes's ear, what seemed like a lifetime ago now. "*Oswick sinks further in danger. The Red King wills to take all for himself. Beware the portals!*" The insect whined like a prophet in trance. "*Seven crystals—you must destroy them all! Aaall...!*"

Madnes opened his eyes, recalling the memory, and stared at the playground's bare soil: the benches, swings, play equipment, along with the grass and trees, all gone.

But then tiny mushrooms and other colorful flora he recognized as indigenous to Wonderland began to sprout and grow, flourishing in place of the playground.

"Whoa, it's like a piece of Wonderland is growing," Harrey marveled. "Look, even the grass is strange colors! I wonder if blue worms will appear?"

"It's not something to be excited about, Harrey," he grumbled under his breath, watching the forested meadow that now replaced the park. The people around panicked, and some ventured to step on the foreign piece of land.

And then, a scream ripped the air.

"My sister, my nephew!" A lady ran across the park space, searching frantically, face wide with tears. "Where are they? They were right here!"

Madnes wished he had an answer, some kind of hope to give her. But everything and everyone who was in the park was gone. He turned aside and let the brim of his hat shield his eyes.

"Are they...?" Harrey asked tentatively as he followed Madnes away from the vanished playground.

"I don't know. Maybe," he replied. If this was just the beginning, then more people and land were going to vanish. And he had no clue as to the cause. You can't stop something without finding what's causing it, first.

"Madnes!"

He tilted his hat back at Alice's call. They watched her trot up to them, once again wearing her cute green skort. "The same thing just happened at a farm across town," she said. "A powerful force is at work. Someone in Wonderland must be doing this."

He looked past her, contemplating. "The Red King wills to take all for himself. Beware the portals... Destroy the seven crystals..."

"Hm?" Alice and Harrey both cocked their heads in question.

"A strange insect told me that. At first I thought it was crazy, like most Wonderland critters are. But now…"

Alice nodded. "Maybe it was foretelling something?"

"Exactly."

"But where could the Red King get the power to do this, and why?"

"Questions we'll have to find answers to, even though there's not much time."

"Get moving then!" Harrey bounced on his heels. "If this keeps up, we won't have an Oswick to come back to."

"Your families," Alice reminded. "You have to warn them and all the people on Oswick."

True. But how?

Through the crowd of mixed terrified and fascinated people, Madnes scanned until he spotted the one person he could use.

"Inspector Coolette!" He trotted over to the stiff man.

"Hatter boy, and other delinquents," the inspector acknowledged them briefly. "Staying out of trouble, I hope?"

Madnes shook his head. "Oswick isn't safe anymore. You must warn everyone." He motioned toward the stand of strange trees and the playground turned into rainbow-meadow.

"Why do you think I'm here?" Coolette sniffed. "We're roping this place off."

A cluster of police fanned out, ropes in hand, beginning to tie off the area from the public.

"That isn't enough. An evacuation needs to be ordered!"

The inspector's thick eyebrows fluttered. "This is an island, boy. Evacuation is no small order and no easy task. Do you really think we have enough boats and airships to carry every human off?" He shook his head briskly. "No, no. That is a last resort. We cannot let ourselves get stirred up by a few odd happenstances." He nodded as if to agree with himself. "Yes, the scientists will come up with an explanation, and then we can think about what course of action to take—if any is needed at all."

"Do you *hear* yourself?" Madnes exclaimed. "A park disappeared and grew back into something you'd only find in a fantasy novel! How can you not panic?"

"My job is to help keep the public in order, Hatter boy— not to get the island residents in a panicked mob that could do further damage. Now go," the inspector shooed with a gloved hand. "Off with you. And no spreading rumors or hysteria."

Madnes shoved open the glass door to his office building, hurrying inside with Alice, Knight Pelur and Harrey on his heels.

Harrey had the orphans in tow, Ash and Drisel, holding hands to keep up.

He knew the inspector was right about one thing: causing island-wide panic wouldn't help matters, especially when there wasn't enough transportation to evacuate everyone quickly. No, what he had to do was stop whatever was causing this. That was his job, and the only way to save Oswick.

If only his mom hadn't been so stubborn, and Harrey's uncle too. They refused to budge an inch from their homes and fly to the mainland, not while there was so much uncertainty about what was happening. A hurricane people understood—they knew the danger and consequences.

But this…no one could understand it, and so, people like his mom refused to leave.

The doorbell announced their entry.

"Madnes! It's about time you got here." There was the gray tabby, pacing back and forth on two booted paws before the counter.

"Cheshire, you're a sight for sore eyes!" Relief flooded through Madnes. Cheshire could fix this problem. Surely he would know what to do, how to set things right. He'd never been more glad to see the cat!

"Hello, Madnes," said a second voice.

Madnes's footsteps faltered before he reached Cheshire. The hair on the back of his neck rose, and his pulse quickened. He lifted his gaze from the cat up to the person standing behind him, swathed in a black frock coat that concealed royal clothes.

The person who had tried to kill him, who almost ended Alice and Ugly Duckling, and who successfully ended Nico's life.

The person whose fault everything was.

Cold rage stormed inside him, ready to be unleashed.

"Oz."

✸36✸

UNEXPECTED

QUEST

For one long second, Madnes glared cold fury at the prince, and Oz likewise stared coolly back.

And then, all heck broke loose.

Before Cheshire could get a word in, Madnes lunged for Oz's throat.

Oz swiftly side-stepped, raising a hand that grew crow talons to cut him as he passed by. But Madnes redirected his momentum and spun around to face the taloned hand — knocking it away with a balled-up fist and leaving Oz open for attack as his other fist struck Oz's cheek.

The force of the blow sent Oz skidding back, crashing into a table and chairs and hitting the far wall.

Cheshire yelped, as Oz staggered to his feet. "Stop, Madnes! This isn't what you think! You can't—"

The cat was ignored. Oz wiped blood from his mouth with a dark grin, then sprouted his crow wings and charged into Madnes, top hat flying off as they hit the floor in a heap.

Black feathers and red-carrot hair mingled in an angry blur.

Cheshire's paws reached out, wanting to stop them but helpless to do so, instead berating them loudly with his voice.

From the sidelines, Harrey called out: "Two points for Madnes! One point for Oz. Another point for Madnes!" Next to him, Knight Pelur held a clipboard, keeping score.

Alice ushered the orphans back and covered their eyes with her hands, no matter how much they begged to watch.

Amidst the turmoil, a shadow fell over the room, and with it two large hands descended: one each grabbing Madnes and Oz by the scruff of their collars and yanking them apart. "How many times do I gotta pull you boys apart, eh?" a familiar voice boomed.

Madnes wiped away blood from a cut above his eyebrow and saw heavy belted boots and the hem of a duster coat. He craned his neck painfully and met the rough stubble face of his uncle; a wide-brim hat played shadows across his jagged features.

Cheshire sank to the floor, exhausted. "Cosmic Hunter! I could not have asked for better timing. Thank you."

Cosmic tossed both Madnes and Oz to the floor, a hand each pressing down on their shoulders to keep them seated. Despite a black eye, the prince kept smirking. Madnes watched angrily as the injuries healed, and felt his own body heal somewhat too.

"Whoa, all that fighting, and they're already healed enough to battle again," marveled Harrey.

"Yes, let's beat each other up for eternity, Madnes." A spark lit in Oz's eyes. "I could use the therapy."

"Ha! If therapy's what you want, how about I give you something that'll really knock you out?" Madnes jabbed a fist—or tried to. His uncle's hand on his shoulder shoved him back down.

"Enough, you rascals! Sheesh." Cosmic shook his head of shaggy black hair.

"Indeed!" Cheshire stepped in, now that the danger of getting caught in the crossfire was past. "You didn't give me a chance to explain things, Madnes. You must learn better control over your emotions. Oswick is at stake, here."

Madnes shut his mouth, halting what he'd been about to say. Adrenaline still pumping, he crossed his legs and crossed his arms, seething but listening. If only Oz would wipe that aggravatingly pleased smirk off his face!

"I'll begin by sharing with you what I've just learned…" Cheshire began, and proceeded with a monologue about the portals, the dangerous state they were in, and what the Red King had planned.

Madnes in turn told about the Forest of the Haunted—glaring sideways at Oz—and of the current situation with the park disappearing and growing back into a garden of Wonderland flora.

"Terraforming spell?" Madnes reviewed Cheshire's information. "Though, I'm not surprised the Red King is bad news, just like his son." He ignored the arrow of hate Oz flung his way.

"Yes, you were spot on in your prediction," Cheshire admitted. "But we have to stop the spell before we can confront him. Time is short."

"You mean, find the seven crystals to break the spell?" said Madnes. "Some Wonderland insect told me the same thing." He considered, then sat up straight. "What's this got to do with Oz? Why is he here, when he's the enemy?" he demanded. The crowv prince's wings and claw were gone, now looking like any other handsome human.

"I told you," the cat sighed, exasperated. "He wants to find the crystals as much as we do, for reasons I promised I would not say. We could use his help, Madnes. We need every little bit we can get for this quest."

"Quest?" Harrey interrupted. "We're calling it a quest, now? Woohoo!" He slung on a backpack crammed with supplies. "We're gonna become famous adventurers! Heroes who saved the world—the sort that people make up songs and ballads for!" he swooned. "I really want my own ballad, something heart-wrenching and epic."

Madnes blocked him out of the conversation with a hand. "You think I can forgive Oz, let alone *trust* him, after what happened to Nico?"

Ash and Drisel were all ears, keeping a distance from the prince and waiting for Cheshire's answer.

The cat looked worn out. "I know this isn't ideal, Madnes. But it's for the sake of Oswick, your home. That is, if you want there to be a home you and your friends can come back to. I don't know what fate will befall the people who live here."

The words hit hard. Madnes kept his lips shut against the tirade writhing inside his chest. His uncle's heavy hand moved to pat his back.

"I'm comin' with ya, lad. Cheer up!" said Cosmic. "Nobody ever saved the world by cryin' and glarin', so pucker up that miserable face of yours."

Madnes rolled his eyes, but he had to agree with his uncle's blunt logic. "Fine." He took a shaky breath, his body still cooling down. "How do we locate these crystals?"

"*Heheh.*" Cosmic pushed the brim of his hat back with a thumb and grinned toothily. "That's why yer feline friend called me here! I know just the person who can help us with that there problem."

⚙37⚙
The White
Duchess

❦

Hidden deep inside an obscure cave, which Cheshire led them to, was a portal resembling a small pond. Its surface swirled and groaned, like an angry whirlpool ready to swallow them whole.

The sight made Madnes question whether this was a good idea or not.

But Cosmic sauntered up, turned, and let himself fall backwards into the swirling blue, just before saying: "This one's stable enough for now, kids. But gettin' back home may be a problem if we fail our quest. Ah well, life's full of risks!"

With that, Uncle vanished beyond the blue.

Madnes swallowed and clenched his fists, not wanting to think about the risk of failure, then dove in after him.

A world of blue, and the chilling feel of ice running along his skin, enveloped him, and then Madnes found himself stumbling out into Wonderland's daylight. He almost lost his footing when the ground rolled and crunched beneath him. After diving into the portal, he'd expected to come out the other side horizontally, but instead, this side of the portal was a vertical swirl in the air, and it spat him out.

He stared down at his boots and the red stuff under them: the ground made of red, porous pebbles. They crunched like cereal when he stepped. The air was salty, and he could hear waves and see a beach far to the left. They were on an island—part of an archipelago of bits of coral trees and red sand

He helped Alice and the orphans as they stumbled out of the vertical rotating portal. Harrey tripped over the crunchy terrain and got a mouthful of red, which he then vigorously spat out. Cheshire, Oz and Pelur strolled forward without a hitch as if they'd stepped onto normal pavement.

Cosmic Hunter was already far ahead, hiking up the red slope toward what resembled a giant seashell. As they got closer, Madnes could see the shell had been carved and made into something like a monastery, with many floors and windows. Its gates were oyster shells, and two fish-like people stood guard.

Cosmic reached them first. He waved one of his hands to the guards and spoke. "Gwee blub bloo blee, fa jeejee ah voo."

Behind him, Harrey guffawed. "Is that really a language?"

"'Course it is!" Cosmic angled his head back. "I'm fluent in all kinds of speech, boy. Comes with the bounty hunter job."

Madnes shook his head.

The fishy guards swung the oyster gates open, and Cosmic led the way inside.

The interior of the palace was the smooth inside of a shell, off-white with hints of pink. A shorter fish person bowed before escorting them down a grand curve-walled hallway.

An oyster door at the end swung open, and they poured into a room of dangling shell lanterns and arched windows. At the head of the room sat a large clam, its white halves closed. No one else seemed to be present besides them.

Madnes absently tugged at the brim of his hat, turning about and wondering what they were supposed to do now, when Cosmic approached the clam, kneeled, and proclaimed.

"White Duchess, greetings! Blee bleu gur. We have come to seek your gracious assistance!"

Alice and Harrey's expressions were as mystified as his own. Had his uncle finally gone insane, speaking to a clam? Was it the destiny of every Hatter? He glimpsed Oz and Cheshire, both blank faced, and Pelur was off trying to munch on the seaweed curtains, muttering something about "too salty." Ash and Drisel wandered here and there, poking at things.

A minute passed, and Cosmic didn't budge one inch before the clam. And then a loud creak came as the clam before them began to open.

It opened like a giant mouth, and a person stood up inside and stretched fin-like arms—a pearl-white fish person, with a long dress and hair like seaweed that swayed as if underwater. Large fish eyes set in a humanoid face regarded Cosmic and then the group behind him.

"A long time I not see you, Cosmic Hunter," she said, and glided out of the clam to alight on the floor. "You brought Madness Solver, I see."

She drew near and circled Madnes slowly. "Normally I not allow people to interrupting my solitary prayer time, but for you I make one exception. Is emergency I hear in your voice and see in your eyes, yes?"

Cosmic nodded, and Cheshire stepped forward, giving the duchess a sweeping bow. "White Duchess, a terrible spell has been cast upon the portals—one that will devastate Earth if not stopped," he explained with grace.

"To surmise, you need location of crystals that are generating this spell?" The fish lady gestured, and a pearl table rose out of the floor, a map engraved across its surface. "Yesss, I have felt disturbances. I wondered what took so long for you to act, Cheshire. You not are on top of things well, lately."

Cheshire bristled, and Madnes hid a grin.

"I would have been, if my apprentice wasn't still a greenhorn."

Madnes grimaced. "So," he spoke and moved to view the table, ignoring the cat, "can you pinpoint where the crystals are for us?"

"Hasty you are." She bopped the tip of his nose with a too-slick finger. "I like that." She grinned, showing fish fangs. "Come and observe." She stretched a webbed hand out over the engraved map, and the group gathered around the table to watch.

Her webbed hand hovered just above the surface, her large eyes turned up to the ceiling. Without looking, she let her hand move across the lands, towns and mountains, feeling for something.

"Yesss, here."

Her hand drew to a halt. Madnes squinted at the village it hovered above.

"This crowv village…somewhere in or somewhere nearby it lay one crystal you looking for. It's closest one, I think."

"Good." Madnes adjusted his hat. "The sooner we destroy it, the quicker that spell will be weakened. Let's go!" He grabbed Pelur's gauntleted wrist, dragging him out with him and away from the curtains.

"Madnes!" Cheshire ran after him, stopping at the oyster door. "You can't be rude! You should at least thank the duchess, first—" But Harrey, Alice and the kids brushed past him, following after. "Oh, honestly! What sort of people is Earth raising you to be? Barbarians?"

Oz lightly dipped his head to the duchess before silently sweeping past the cat, black frock swishing.

"Dash it all!" Cheshire grumbled, and gave a deep bow to the duchess. Her fish lips held amusement. "Time is of the essence, I suppose."

"Is true. Safe quest I hope you have." She waved her webbed fingers.

Pelur, in grand dragon form, carried the motley group from the archipelago across to Wonderland mainland. His keen dragon eyes followed the landscape, pinpointing the hilly rainforest and its hidden crowv village which the White Duchess had marked out on the map for them.

Bird calls and monkey howls echoed the trees as the dragon descended into pines and mist.

The passengers slid off Pelur's scaly back to the spongy floor.

Alice shook her head of golden hair, shaking off pine needles. Drisel spotted an orange, fluffy squirrel and scampered after it down an overgrown path.

"Wait, Drisel!" Alice moved to chase after, but Madnes motioned that he would get her.

His footsteps muffled by the loamy ground, Madnes caught up and snatched Drisel by the shoulders. She dangled her feet in the air, pleading and giggling as he swung her around. "Stay with the group, you rascal," he said, and plopped her down.

She grinned and pointed an excited finger up ahead to where rows of thatch houses and tents made up a village in the middle of the forest.

"The crowv!"

❈38❈

VILLAGE IN THE FOREST

"The crystal must be somewhere nearby," Madnes spoke once the rest of the group had caught up and gathered round.

Alice nodded. "Right. But will they tell us where it is?"

"If they know, they'll tell *me*." Oz swept past them, gliding down the narrow path leading into the village.

Black wings materialized from his back, making him look every inch a dark prince.

Not to be left behind, Madnes grunted and hurried after him.

With no fence or guards to halt them, they strode easily past several thatch and tent structures. The villagers paused in their chores when they caught sight of the strangers.

Madnes swallowed. They looked almost human, as Oz did, except for black wings sprouting out of their backs, and some had black feathers mixed in with their hair.

Madnes also noted how frail and gaunt most of them appeared, malnourished compared to Oz. They watched their group like stunned deer at first; one crowv stirring the contents of a boiling cauldron paused, the spoon half raised.

Oz came to a halt at the village center, near the heating cauldron and a central stone well. He turned with a flourish of his long coat to face the gathering crowd of crowv.

"It has been too long since my last visit," Oz spoke. "How do I find you?"

One crowv ventured to step forward, an elderly man with graying frayed wings. "You find us well, Prince Oz." He wobbly bowed a knee, using a staff. "You honor us with your presence and your concern."

It was strange to see Oz treated as a prince—the once normal child who loved books and used to laugh at his jokes.

Madnes wanted to add some words of his own, but felt a burly hand on his arm, Uncle Cosmic motioning that he keep quiet. "This is Oz's territory," he whispered, "Leave the talkin' to him."

Madnes grumbled but complied.

"And what of the illness?" questioned Oz. "How has the village's health been?"

The elder wet his lips. "Come to the head house, Your Highness. I think it best we speak there."

The head house was a thatch-and-mud piece of work, with a fire pit at the center and small window holes letting in air. The elder, Morak, motioned them to sit on a ring of pillows surrounding the pit, a kettle heating above the ashes.

Morak explained to them that an illness without a name had been ravaging the crowv people across Wonderland, in villages such as this one, and though it had slowed for several years, the death toll was once again on the rise. The same illness that had taken the life of Oz's mother.

"Your mom passed away?" Madnes blurted out, shocked.

Conversation paused, Cheshire, Pelur and the elder glancing at him.

Oz didn't meet his gaze, instead staring off at nothing, tight-lipped.

"Why didn't you tell me?" Madnes faced Oz anyway. "I knew she was ill, and heard that was the reason why your family had moved away, to find her treatment, but…"

He couldn't get the rest of the words out.

Oz's brow furrowed. "Save your pity for yourself." His voice lowered. "You're the last person I want remorse from."

The words stung, but Madnes held his silence.

It was Cheshire who next brought up the topic of the Terraforming spell, and a crystal having been detected somewhere nearby.

The elder scratched the side of his scraggly cheek. "I've not heard of any such thing found here…but by all means, you are free to search the village as you please. We will not refuse you anything you wish, Prince Oz." He dipped his head.

Oz slightly nodded in return, the black feathers in his hair rustling. "We will do just that, and also scour the outer perimeters," Oz decided.

"The surrounding forest?" Morak's behavior turned worried, his taloned feet fidgeting. "It is bad luck to go far from the village, Your Highness. Those who do, show signs of the illness very quickly. It lurks out there..." His wrinkly throat rippled as he swallowed.

Oz's expression hardened, as if changing his mind about something. "I want to find the source," he said suddenly. "Cheshire, you and your group can search for the crystal as you like, but in the meantime, I am going to hunt down this illness." His jaw set and he rose from the pillows. "Let me know when the crystal is found."

Madnes stared after him, lips parted. He could almost see remnants of his former friend there, in that brief instant. Oz cared about his people—as cold and heartless as he'd been towards Madnes and his friends, he was different here among Wonderlanders, if still icy around the edges.

'It's just me he hates.'

"No, please, Your Highness! Do not put yourself at risk!" The elder rose and made as if to stop his prince.

"It is my decision to make, Morak," Oz stated firmly. It was clear he would not be swayed.

"Do not go far, then. You must avoid going too near the river. Those who are dying of the illness go there, never to return."

"A river? You don't fish?" Madnes had to ask. "Your people look like they're starving. I'd think fishing would be a great—"

"No, no," Morak exclaimed. "Anyone who goes that far will catch death! Instead, we hunt the nearby trees for birds and larva. It is not enough food for us, no," he admitted grimly, "but better to go hungry than die in such a terrible way."

Oz hesitated for only a second. "I don't believe in bad luck. If you say going outside the village perimeters is how crowv have been catching this illness, then there must be a tangible explanation—a source that I can track down." His gray eyes narrowed. "I'm surprised Father hasn't sent more people to investigate this matter. I thought it was an inborn illness, something genetic that crowv were susceptible to...but now it sounds nothing of the sort."

"It's too dangerous, Your Highness." Morak pleaded. "And it may pose a threat to non-crowv as well, if any of you should venture too far."

"Why don't you just abandon this forest, and move somewhere else?" Harrey suggested, for once sounding logical.

Morak fixed him with a look that said Harrey clearly did not understand. "The bad luck follows with us. It does not matter where we go, Earthian. We cannot escape it."

"It *follows* you?" Cheshire's ears flattened. "How is that possible? If you catch it from your environment, then moving somewhere else should put a stop to it."

The wheels in Madnes's mind started turning, eager to solve the mystery. "Something *more* is going on. But we'll have to risk going out there to learn *what*."

"Stop putting your nose where it doesn't belong," growled Oz. "This is my job. Make yourself useful and go find that crystal."

Madnes stiffened.

The prince glided past his shoulder without so much as a glance.

Madness held in the terse remark waiting on the tip of his tongue.

⚙39⚙

MYSTERY AT THE RIVER

"Right, then!" Cheshire clapped his paws together. "Spread out and search the village for the crystal, but don't go venturing past the border," he warned their group. "We don't know if the illness poses a threat to non-crowv or not."

As the motley group dispersed, Madnes tiptoed away...though not before a sharp "Madnes!" from the cat caught him. "Where do you think you're off to?" demanded the feline.

Madnes put on an impish look and winked over his shoulder. "Off to get into trouble, of course. See you later!"

Hand firmly on his hat, Madnes dashed out of sight.

"Don't go beyond the village!" Cheshire tried to call after him, but it was no use. His whiskers trembled and his furry cheeks fumed. "Why do Madness Solvers *never* listen?"

Madnes peeked one eye around the mossy bark of a pine. He trailed after Oz, who followed a crowv guide beyond the village perimeters. The forest slopped downhill, a stumbling terrain of hidden rocks, moss, and gnarled roots. After a while, the guide came to a halt and turned back to the prince.

"This is as far as we should risk going, My Prince," he bowed. "The river is close, the bad luck is near." His neck craned like a nervous bird, watching their surroundings.

Oz nodded lightly. "Yes, you should go back."

"But, My Prince—!"

Oz raised his hand in gesture for silence. "I command it," he said. "Do not fear. I will not put myself at unnecessary risk. But I do intend to locate the source of this illness that's been taking my people. That is the job of a ruler: to take care of their subjects, is it not?"

The crowv stared at him, jaw working for words and finding none.

"Now, go," ordered Oz. "Leave the rest to me. I will return before nightfall."

The overwhelmed crowv bowed, and with reluctance made his way back uphill.

"Quite a show of bravery, there, going off alone. Or is it that you can't stand to be around people for too long?" Madnes hopped from behind the tree, landing several feet from Oz. He watched Oz's face turn from surprise to anger and pure annoyance.

"Do my claws need to come out and slice that nose off, which seems so terribly fond of sticking itself into other people's business?"

"Ha!" Madnes strolled past the prince, folding his arms and raising his chin high. "As the Madness Solver, it's my job to solve mysteries and promote peace," he said. "And so, I plan on solving this case, with or without you."

Madnes stumbled over a rock and had to lower his chin to watch the ground. His foot passed a curious patch of fungus growing on a root.

Oz hissed through his teeth, loose strands of hair falling into his eyes. "I'm solving it first!"

Madnes gave him an impish chuckle, and then he raced headlong down the forested hill.

"Oh no you don't," Oz shouted, chasing after him. "I'm not letting you beat me!"

Madnes nimbly kept ahead of Oz, taunting him all the way down. That is, until the rush of water reached his ears and he scrambled to a stop.

Oz plowed into his back, and they both spilled out of the forest and onto a sandy riverbank.

Madnes tried to raise his head, Oz's weight crushing him.

The river? Uh-oh. They weren't supposed to have come this close. He struggled to rise, and Oz deliberately took his time getting up—pushing off his back so Madnes got a mouthful of sand.

Madnes scrambled up, spitting, ready to grab Oz from behind and rub a handful of sand all over his perfect head. But Oz stood frozen, his gaze fixed on something.

Madnes dusted his hands off and moved to his side to catch whatever Oz was looking at.

Bones—a stretch of skeletons littered the riverbank as far as the terrain would let them see before the river curved around a rising cliff face.

Madnes stepped closer, inspecting the bones. The surfaces were black, and pockmarked as if by acid.

"The illness," Oz murmured behind his left shoulder.

"Or is it?" Madnes questioned. "Can an illness really follow a village around?"

The prince straightened and spread his black wings with a rustling flap.

"Wait—take me with you," Madnes quickly said.

"As if I'd carry your sorry backside around," Oz snorted, and lifted off. Before he got more than a foot off the sand, Madnes grabbed him by the ankles and wrapped his arms around Oz's knees.

"Let go, you backstabber!" Oz kicked and flapped above the bank.

"Stop bringing up the past, and just fly!" urged Madnes, somehow his top hat staying on his head. "Check beyond that cliff."

Muttering something bitter under his breath, Oz flapped his wings and glided around the cliff face, following the river.

After several yards, the river ran abruptly into the foot of a steep waterfall.

Madnes narrowed his gaze, focused on something like a cave behind the water cascade. He voiced his findings to Oz, who then lowered them to the nearest bank.

Madnes let go and landed on the sand. "Just for the record, not agreeing with you on every single thing when we were kids is not called backstabbing." He huffed and readjusted his hat over his dampened bangs.

Oz barked a laugh. "Is that all it was to you? You ran away from me when I needed your help most, and you don't call that betrayal?"

Madnes kicked at the sand, turning his back away. "I'm sorry you took it that way. But you were acting so strange, and I was a frightened child. It wasn't that I didn't want to be there for you, I just…all those crazy things you were saying about your mom and another world and danger…I was afraid."

"Things that were all true." Oz's teeth gritted. "And you didn't bother to let me even prove it to you!"

Oz shoved Madnes's back, knocking him to the ground so that he got a mouthful of dirt this time. "My mother went missing, and you could've helped me find her. But you didn't. You left me, like a coward. It was your fault!"

"How cwan you bwame mwe?" Madnes spat out dirt. "That illness kwilled her—not me!"

Oz snarled near his ear. But before either of them could move, the ground beneath them rumbled…

…And cracked open.

Madnes sucked in a breath of dirt and air as he tumbled, headfirst, into an opening sinkhole.

Gripping Madnes by his jacket, Oz tumbled in after, dragged along into sudden darkness.

❀40❀

Oz's True Goal

Everything became the sensation of falling into darkness...and then the sudden impact with ground drove the air out of Madnes's lungs. There was the rushing sound of falling dirt, and bits of rock pelted his back for a moment longer, and then all became silent.

Using the brim of his hat to shield his eyes, Madnes tried to adjust to the encompassing darkness around him. From the glow of daylight at the sinkhole's mouth above, he could make out what looked like a tunnel stretching off into the dark before him. He crawled towards it, assessing the area; he'd fallen through the collapsed portion of an underground tunnel—man-made, judging by the tall, rectangular contour.

A dark shape crawled up beside him. Oz shook off dirt from his wings before vanishing them into his back. "What is a tunnel doing here?" He surveyed.

"My question exactly." Madnes pushed to his feet, and coughed on a cloud of dust as he did. "Time to go exploring." He started into a trot down the dark tunnel.

Not to be outdone, Oz followed after him, shielding his mouth with a sleeve.

Madnes's vision gradually adjusted to the dark. The dirt tunnel surfaces soon gave way to hard metal, and their boots *clinked* at every step.

Other than that, there was no sound down here. The quiet was unnerving and awkward.

Madnes took the chance to finish what he'd been meaning to say. "I'm angry with you, Oz, and I can't brush off the things you did. But I'm also worried about you."

"Here you go again," Oz huffed irritably. "Can't we walk in silence?"

"What darkness has taken hold of you, Oz? What made you change so much?" Madnes persisted.

"Darkness? You mean that Syn fairytale?" Oz barked a cold laugh. "Typical Madnes Hatter. Blame it on some mysterious force because it can't possibly be anything else."

"Then what *did* change you? And don't act like it was all my fault."

"...I don't think I changed so much as I learned," said Oz. "Learned the cold ways of reality. You can't count on others, especially friends. They act like they'll always be there for you, but when the time comes that you need them most, they vanish, walk away, leave you behind."

Madnes rolled his eyes. "So, you *are* blaming me."

"No. Thanks to you, I was able to grow up independent, become someone who doesn't need to rely on others. What I do blame you for is not helping me find my real mother the day she went missing."

"But I *saw* her! She was standing right there beside you that day—looking and acting the same as ever, except for being ill," argued Madnes. "You were convinced she was some imposter—a robotic replica that your real mother had been switched with. But I couldn't see it, Oz. I couldn't believe you. Then the next thing I knew, you and your family had moved away from Oswick…" He paused and exhaled. "Now, I hear your mother had died. A robot *can't* die, Oz." Madnes stuffed his hands in his pockets.

"She was a robot—a fake—pretending to be ill and die. I *know* it wasn't my real mother…" Oz murmured bitterly.

"Then what's that got to do with seeking the Madness Solver power? Hurting my friends to get to me? You do realize that your father only wanted you to become the next Madness Solver so that he could have that power—you—under his control, and not have someone like me out here ruining his schemes?"

"I have my own reasons for wanting it. And it has nothing to do with the king." Oz raised his chin. "As for hurting your friends, it was the quickest way to make you use up your power. I know your secret; I know all about what will happen once the clock on your wrist turns full circle."

"And you want that for yourself?" Madnes stared at him, incredulous. "You want to die young, like I will?"

"The end result is worth it," Oz stated, marching on as Madnes's steps faltered and slowed.

"That's *it*…" Madnes halted, staring after the crowv prince with sudden realization. "*That's* what you've been doing, all this time."

Oz paused and turned halfway to look back at him, gaze icy yet with a hint of wariness beneath the surface.

"You're *still* looking for her. You believe your mother is still alive somewhere. That's why you want this power—to find her."

Oz's mouth hung slack, and Madnes knew he'd hit the mark.

A frosty mask made Oz expressionless once more, and the prince marched on.

"Why didn't you tell me?" Madnes continued. "Instead of hurting my friends, ruining Nico's life, just to get this power, why didn't you ask for my help?" He marched after him. "Did you think I wouldn't listen or care?"

"As if I would *ever* ask you," growled Oz. "You didn't believe me when I first told you my mother had been replaced by a fake. So why would you believe me years later? No, I don't need help from you. I can solve my own problems."

"You *idiot*." Madnes rushed him from behind, catching Oz with an arm hooked around the neck. Oz fought to get free, jabbing his elbows back into Madnes's ribs. But Madnes ignored the pain, holding him. "You bat-blind, porridge-headed idiot! If you had told me, back when you came to visit Oswick, I would have believed you and been willing to help!"

"Yes, now that you've seen Wonderland, seen the impossible, you're willing to believe your ex-best friend," Oz spat.

"I'm sorry I was afraid; I'm sorry I chose not to believe you back then. I can't change the past! But I *can* do something now." He suddenly let go, and Oz stumbled forward, rubbing his collar. "If you say she's still alive somewhere, then I'm going to find your mother," Madnes stated, passing him by. "With or without you."

Madnes ran down the metallic tunnel, and Oz, breathless with shock, started after him. "What? Wait! You can't just— Madnes!!"

❀41❀

ᴛRACED ᴛO ᴛHE

SOURCE

Oz's vision adjusted to the darkness as he pursued Madnes. The energetic human was soon out of sight. And when the tunnel's metallic, dust-encrusted surface came to a sudden dead end, Oz's boots skidded to a stop.

Before him rose a metal door contraption—bolts, locks and gears holding it shut.

How was this supposed to open? Where had that Madnes gone off to? He was sure there were no other tunnels but this one. So, where was he?

Oz drew close, inspecting the door's mechanisms.

No trace of a keyhole to be found; it must open some other way…

A gear turned. Locks and bolts released.

The door was suddenly opening.

Heart thumping, Oz ducked to the left, pressing his body flat against the tunnel wall.

"Oz, *pssst*! What are you doing?"

Oz blinked at the human peeking around the now-open metal door, Madnes flashing him a smug grin before disappearing.

He'd already gotten inside? How had Madnes unlocked the…?

Oz growled and slipped in after him. It must be thanks to the power's knowledge that he'd gotten the door open.

A cool gust blew hair back from his temples as he stepped inside. The glow from light rods, spaced along the walk and ceiling, cast the atmosphere in a greenish haze. A grated floor scuffed under his boots, and a musty scent hung in the air with traces of something bitter.

Oz let his eyes scan the space and its branching paths. Equipment lay everywhere. Conduits laced the walls like tree roots around faintly beeping boxes.

He drew close to one of the luminous green boxes and leaned toward the glass. A spongey substance was growing inside, like a green fungus, and tiny particles like powder covered it—a dusty, glowing powder.

"There's the source of your illness."

Oz whipped his head around. Madnes stepped up, hands in pockets. "I wasn't sure at first, but getting a good look at it now, I'm certain this dusty powder is what's making the crowv ill," said Madnes.

Oz examined the particles once more. "What makes you so sure?"

"I spotted this fungus growing on rocks and tree bark, back when we made our way down to the river," Madnes explained. The glow cast greenish shadows across his features. "Some had this same yellowish powder; and it doesn't look natural, if you ask me."

"Is the Madness Solver telling you this?"

He shrugged his shoulders. "If a crowv brushes against this, they catch ill. That's what I think."

"Why is this being cultivated and planted in the forest? Does someone want the crowv to die out?" Oz started to fume. He pulled back from the glass and continued down the grated path.

Madnes hesitated before following.

The path led to an open circular doorway, and Oz didn't hesitate to go through. But the sight beyond hit him like a wall of bricks, and his built-up anger paled.

A cavernous space stretched before them, and lined in neat rows throughout were glass caskets. Conduits ran to them, and little lights lit up a face inside each one.

Oz stumbled backwards before falling to his knees, going numb all over. It was Madnes who went to the nearest glass casket and peered inside. "Ah..." Oz could hear the heaviness in Madnes's voice, "*Now* everything makes sense."

Gritting his jaw until it ached, Oz forced himself up and went to where the human stood. Inside the casket was what he feared to see—what was inside each of these caskets, rows upon rows of them. A face, eyes closed in death, and the hum of conduits surrounding a crowv body.

"Those black patches," Madnes pointed them out on the body's skin. "They match what we saw on the bones by the riverbed."

"What..." it was an effort to speak. "What are they doing to my people?" Oz growled. "Who is doing this?"

Madnes bent down, tapping the cords and conduits on the underside of the raised casket. "These are syphoning something from the body. Tell me, do crowv have special powers or something like magic in them?"

Oz took a moment before he could think. "Yes. It's not magic, like what you're thinking, but a power in our genes. It's what makes us crowv and able to transform. Why? You think it's being syphoned out?"

"Yes." Madnes straightened. "I'm thinking the illness is a clever ploy to collect crowv bodies for whatever work is being done here. Think about it," he faced him. "When a crowv falls ill, they leave the village so as not to spread the illness to anyone else. They leave to die, most likely coming down to the riverbed for water and comfort. They're weak and alone, and that's when they get captured and brought down here to this lab. It's like the perfect crime. No one expects them to come back, so no one ever goes looking or discovers the truth."

Oz's muscles tightened. "And that's how the illness can follow a village, even after it moves. The people running this laboratory can plant the illness wherever they like and scare the crowv into thinking their surroundings are cursed!" He stepped back from the casket, his vision taking in the many rows filling the cavernous hall. "They were killed for their power... How many *years* has this gone on? How much power? And for *what*?" His chest burned. "When I find the one responsible for this..."

"A Terraforming spell's crystal is nearby." Madnes hesitated, hand raking his bangs back under his hat. "This…could be connected to it."

Oz looked at him sharply. "Are you saying this was all to generate those crystals and the spell?"

"…I'm afraid so. Gathering up power, over the course of however many years, to create seven crystals." His eyes shut, pained. "I guess they're just gathering back-up power, now. Not much other reason to keep running this place."

Oz bit his lip so hard it bled.

Father wanted the Terraforming spell. Did he know at what cost it was being made? Did he knowingly use Oz's people—his mother's people—to do this? Were the crowv nothing to him but a source of power to be used?

'Mother…where are you?' Hot tears stung his eyes.

✢42✢
Do Away With

Oz stared at the caskets—his murdered people—anger writhing through his soul.

Father would pay for this. Oh yes, he would pay.

"Come on, Oz." Madnes urged him. "The crystal must be close by. There's nothing more you can do for them now." His glance indicated the dead.

"Oh, I wouldn't be so sure of that," Oz uttered darkly. He trailed after Madnes into the next room over.

A metal contraption, like a giant container, filled this cramped room, and Madnes skirted around it.

"I'm not sure what the crystal will look like—I mean, I think it'll be something crystal-ish," said Madnes. "But— Hey, what are you doing?"

Oz spread his wings and flapped up to the top of the giant metal contraption, which rumbled and hummed with syphoned crowv power. Several levers poked out from its bulging surface and Oz grabbed hold of one, yanking it down.

"Oz! What are you—?" Madnes started.

The lab's greenish lights flickered. The humming shifted to a steaming gurgle.

Something beeped, and a sign flashed red: *Warning*.

"You're overloading it," he exclaimed.

"A nice bomb to wipe out this place, don't you think?" Oz landed back down.

"Sure, except we need to find that crystal before it does!"

"Get your Madness Solver backside moving, then."

Their footsteps clamored down the next tunnel, and between Oz's and Madnes's strength, they wrenched the next locked door open, creaking it inward.

A circular room lay beyond. Gadgets and beeping things lined the curving wall, with people in hazmat suits attending them. But most noticeable out of everything was the gleaming diamond-shaped crystal at the room's center, raised on a platform.

"Easier to find than I thought," Madnes commented. "But with that alarm going off, there are people everywhere. We need to distract—"

"*Graaah!*" Oz charged ahead, both hands elongated and darkening into claws. He slashed left and right, plowing through the lab workers like grass.

"Or we could just do that," Madnes finished and shook his head. "We can't leave them here with the bomb, though."

"Keep them alive, after what they've done?" Oz turned, veins throbbing, the last of the workers downed to the floor. "These are murderers!"

"Your hands aren't exactly clean, either. Don't pretend you're better than them," Madnes shot back, and Oz stared for a second before looking away. "They'll be punished— don't worry about that. And maybe they'll be of use to us, too," he added.

Oz shifted his anger to the crystal, claws raised.

Mother wasn't here. The crowv woman must be inside a different crystal, not this one. He charged, knife claws wide.

At first, he'd planned to betray Madnes's group and fight to save the crystals from being destroyed. He didn't care about Oswick or Earth's Terraforming destruction. He had only come along on this trip to find Mother.

But now, after learning what had happened to the crowv, he wanted to obliterate every speck of these cursed crystals and everything the king had planned.

He slashed, claws striking the crystalline surface with a screeching ring.

Oz landed and turned to eye his handiwork, only to find that the crystal was still there—whole and unblemished.

Madnes charged next, throwing all his weight into a flying side kick through the sparkling rock.

But there wasn't so much as a shatter under his boot, and the force of the kick sent him stumbling back instead.

"The crowv power inside the crystal is too strong. We can't break it like this," Madnes panted.

"I doubt the explosion will affect it, either." Oz let his claws retreat, hands human once more.

Madnes wrapped his arms around the base, lifting the crystal up. "A little help here?" he said, arms strained around the slippery load.

"Seriously? That's your genius plan?" Oz snorted.

"Well, it's either that or we die while trying to think up something else. I don't know about you, but I'm not keen on exploding."

Oz rolled his eyes and reached for the crystal, only to have Madnes throw its full weight at him. "Take care of that, will you? I'll drag these people out." Madnes trotted off.

Oz growled around the crystal, though it sounded more like a grunt. Between the crystal's weight and time running out, he left arguing for later and began a hurried run toward the red blinking word *Exit* above a door.

The world went dark for a moment past the exit, as it followed through a carved-out cave. Then light appeared from an open rock mouth, and he came out into afternoon sunshine. The din of rushing water hit his ears, and drippings from the rock ceiling quickly plastered his hair. He was standing behind a waterfall—the same one they'd seen earlier.

Oz sidestepped along a ledge leading from the right of the watery cascade—not easy to do while bearing a huge crystal nearly his own size.

He was almost to the riverbank when the ledge beneath him rumbled.

He craned his neck to look back, watching as smoke began frothing out of the cave mouth and into the waterfall. His forehead creased while he waited.

A top hat emerged, followed by Madnes streaking out of the cave and into the waterfall. Clothes smoking; arms, shoulders and back burdened with a pile of unconscious workers.

The rumbling intensified, and flames burst from the cave just short of Madnes, as the giant container underground exploded. Oz watched as they all fell into the river, and then Madnes struggled to grab everyone to shore.

"He should have been named Idiotnes instead of Madnes," he muttered. He watched curls of flame and smoke rise from underground.

'Good riddance.'

Oz huffed and went to help "Idiotnes" recapture the lab workers.

❈43❈

REVISED PLAN

"The crowv can't stay here—not with that chemical powder spread about the forest," Madnes said around a bowl of green pea stew.

The night encircled the group seated around one of several fire pits in the crowv village as the meal was served.

"Agreed. I'm sure the White Duchess won't mind taking them under her care, temporarily." Cheshire's whiskers twitched. "If that's all right with you, prince?"

Oz's brow furrowed. "I don't see any other options," came his tart reply.

Madnes shot a frown in Oz's direction and shifted his pillow seat toward Pelur. The dragon knight was busy swallowing down whole cabbages and pea pods. "Pelur, do you think you can carry the lab prisoners and help guide the crowv back to the duchess?"

The knight nodded, mouth too stuffed to speak, like a chipmunk preparing for winter.

"Well, we now know how ol' Red King powered up his Terraforming spell," Cosmic Hunter spoke around a twig toothpick, an arm propped over his knee. "Who'd a thought such a scheme was goin' on? Downright evil." He took out a knife from one of his belts and began sharpening its edge.

"There are many other villages," the elder crowv spoke. Weariness lined his voice now, after having listened to their grim discovery. "They are most likely living under the same threat as us, My Prince. You must help them."

Madnes shifted his gaze back to Oz. It was clear the prince was conflicted over something, but he gave the elder a curt nod. "Of course. They will be taken care of," Oz assured. His gaze didn't meet the crowv's but went past, as if distracted by something only he could see.

"Speaking of threat," Harrey interrupted, still chewing. "There're six more crystals out there, and time's running out fast. How're we gonna find them all before our home's gone?"

The same thought had been crossing Madnes's mind. He didn't like what he was about to suggest, but like Oz had said: options were limited.

"I think we should split up," said Madnes.

Silence rolled around the fire pit.

He looked around.

While no one's expression disagreed with him, none seemed eager about the idea either. "It's not ideal, I know," he admitted, "but we can cover more ground that way. Each group will meet back at the duchess's palace once they have their crystal."

Cosmic grinned around the toothpick. "Sounds good t' me, boy."

Harrey agreed, eager for adventure, though Alice beside him looked hesitant through the fire's light.

"Splitting up is ridiculous. Dangerous." Oz's knuckles cracked.

Madnes didn't bother facing Oz, instead casting an agitated smirk to the sky. "Let me guess, Oz. You don't want any of us to find your mother before you do, because you're paranoid and fear that we'll bake a crow pie or something."

Oz set his hands on his hips angrily. "How do I know you won't use her to blackmail me?"

"We don't have time to indulge your untrusting nature, Oz. And I'd never want to try crow pie—believe me. Too many feathers."

Oz rolled his eyes and made a sound through his teeth.

"We have to hurry while there's still an Oswick left to save," Madnes stressed. "You'll have to decide for yourself what you want to do, Oz: help relocate the many other crowv out there or search for the crystals and your mother."

Oz's glare came ice hot.

"We don't have time to help the crowv. But we can help your mother if she's with one of those spell crystals. Go help your people, Oz. Leave your mother to us, and come join in the search as soon as you can."

Without a word, the prince rose and left the fire pit, dark coat fading into the night. Cosmic continued sharpening his arsenal, and Harrey got a second helping of pea stew.

"Too bad nothing's worked to break that crystal you guys brought back," Harrey mentioned. "We've tried just about everything! What's with it? How're we supposed to stop the spell if we can't even destroy them?"

Madnes listened as Cheshire answered. "A power greater than, or equal to, what's been stored inside that crystal is the only thing that can destroy it, I fear. As to how we'll find something like that…" furry shoulders lifted, "I am not sure."

Propped against the wooden wall of the guest's hut, the crystal gleamed beneath the moonlight playing across its many facets and angles.

Alice glanced every which way before approaching it. Most everyone was still back at the fire pits, eating.

Alice could feel the hum in the air, the energy, the song of the crystal's power. She drew nearer, nearer, gaze fixed on the glassy surface and shimmering facets within.

Her body hummed in tune with its song, and a glow like sunlight pulsed underneath her skin, lighting up like a thousand fireflies in the night.

She reached out, compelled to touch the crystal.

So smooth, alive, powerful…

Kr—KRtch!

A crack webbed through the crystal's heart—from tip to base.

And it split apart.

Alice backed away and gaped, surprised to find the crystal split in two, its power gone.

'It worked. I can break them,' she thought with a thrill.

She could stop the crystals.

Something behind her rustled. Alice spun around and faced a shadow as it melted into Oz.

'Oh no, he saw me!'

A second shadow approached, melting into Madnes.

Both boys looked from her to the crystal and back.

"What did you do?"

❀44❀

SOME GIRLS ARE

A MYSTERY

They saw Alice—and the crystal laid cracked in two before her.

"What did you do? *How?* That crystal's tougher than a leviathan's hide!" said Madnes, impressed by the damage.

Alice shied away like a frightened doe.

"How could *you* break that crystal when nothing else could?" Oz demanded to know, suspicion written in his posture. "What *are* you?"

Alice shuffled backwards, and he took a step nearer.

"Nothing has power like that. Nothing but a sorceress." Oz's gray gaze narrowed. "Is that what you are? A wicked sorceress?"

"No!" she cried desperately.

Oz took another step but Madnes's arm rose, blocking his chest. "Enough. This is Alice we're talking about. Of course, she isn't a sorceress," he rebuked.

"Then explain your power, girl," snapped Oz. "You're not human. I could sense Wonderland aura surrounding you while that crystal broke."

Madnes blocked the prince from getting close, but there was no denying his words.

Madnes met Alice's gaze, sending an unspoken plea that she say something, that she not hide secrets. But he remembered his promise to her: that he would never ask about her secrets.

He thought he could be fine with that, tried to be fine with that, but...

Alice took one more step back before she turned and sprinted into the dark of night.

"Explain yourself!" Oz shouted and shoved Madnes's arm aside. But Madnes blocked him again, refusing to let him chase after her.

"She's *my* friend. I'll take responsibility for her," he faced Oz's suspicious glare. "She's not a threat to you, I promise. If anything, she's been of help."

With his chance to pursue her gone, Oz relented. "For now, maybe. But if that changes..." He let the warning go unsaid.

"You'll let me handle things," Madnes hardened his tone.

"Just as the crowv are your people to manage, my friends and anyone who calls Earth home are *my* people."

For several drawn seconds they stared each other down. Then Oz sniffed and turned aside. "Don't take that responsibility lightly," he warned over a shoulder and ducked inside one of the crowv huts for the night.

Madnes shut his eyes, the light from many fire pits playing afterimages across his vision. *'Fairy?'* He reached out with his mind.

It had been a long time since the Madness Solver power within him had spoken. *'Can you hear me?'* he tried. A fickle creature she was, but one with vast knowledge he needed. Since he was forced to be her host, he should get some sort of benefit, right?

'I need your knowledge, fairy. Can you tell me: what is Alice? You must be able to sense what she is, how she broke the crystal?'

He waited. Something glowed white in the dark recesses of his mind, a flutter of purple gossamer wings.

Hmm~ Yes, I do know.

There she was, voice like a hum in his ears. *But why should I tell you?*

'She's my friend,' he answered. *'Please, tell me the truth. How can I protect her unless I know?'*

You would have me betray such a valuable secret? the fairy scoffed. *Ha! How greedy of you, Madnes.* She tsked, almost mockingly. *I refuse.*

He gritted his teeth. This fairy could be so irritating.

'But I—'

You keep her safe by staying ignorant of it, human. She cut him off. *Stop asking questions and leave her alone.* The fairy paused for a moment, then adding: *Make sure Oz and everyone else leaves her alone, as well.*

Valuable secret? Keep her safe by staying ignorant?

The fairy fell silent, gone back to wherever she resided within him. Madnes itched with curiosity, the desire for knowledge. But if it would keep Alice safe, then he would try to resist the urge to know.

However, if she was the only person who could destroy the crystals, then how could he keep that a secret from everyone else?

Dawn crested the tree-obscured horizon, and the group was already gulping down a breakfast of acorn bread and herbal cheese before starting the journey ahead.

Cheshire was first to spot the crystal mysteriously cracked, and soon everyone was buzzing about it.

Madnes didn't see Alice among them but spotted her hiding at the edge of the village tree line.

"It was me," Madnes confessed to the crowd gathered near a boiling pot of eggs over the fire pit. "I kept working at it, and then the power inside me suddenly doubled and the crystal broke." He said it as authentically as he could and, based on their awed reaction, it worked.

"You're just full of surprises, ain't ya, boy?" Cosmic slapped his back.

"*Ak*—Yes," he coughed. "I'm still new to this Madness Solver power business."

"Wowee! What else you can do, Madnes? Maybe we should test some stuff..." Harrey studied him like a new invention.

Madnes cringed and backed away. "Um, no thanks."

"By the way, how are we gonna do this whole quest thing? How's our group gonna be split up?"

Madnes combed a hand back through his hair, top hat in other hand. "I've been thinking it over," he began.

He spied Alice approaching from the trees, now that he'd taken credit for the crystal in her place. He sent her a reassuring glance. "So, here's what I've decided…"

❄45❄

ON THE MOVE

A red light flashed across the monitor screen.
The advisor stumbled over his own squat legs in his
hurry, racing to see the cause.

One of the seven crystals on the monitor had suddenly
gone red, reading: *Power Connection Terminated*.

"What in the blazes?" He drew up the digital file, and all
the readings on that particular crystal had, indeed, gone
dead.

"Not good, not good... His Majesty won't like this."

"It must be the work of that new Madness Solver, and his ever-meddlesome cat mentor." The Red King steepled his fingers, observing the portal readings throughout Wonderland via the video screen embedded in his royal desk. "But what gave the location of that specific crystal away?"

"Perhaps," the advisor suggested, "they were investigating the crowv village nearby, and stumbled upon the lab?"

The king exhaled an icy breath, and the air in the room chilled. "And what is the probability of that?" he demanded. "If they've found a way to locate the Terraforming spell's crystals, then I cannot sit back and do nothing—especially when it seems they've found a way to destroy them."

"Of course not, Your Majesty," the advisor agreed, hoping to stave off the king's fury. "Shall I send the word throughout Wonderland, then?"

"Yes. Along with the best of my knights." The king twisted his dark beard between his fingers, his other hand gripping the wooden chair arm carved in the shape of bowing dragons.

"Pardon, Majesty, but how do you think they destroyed such a crystal?" the advisor ventured to ask.

The king's eyes blazed, and he flinched back.

"The nymph of the Madness Solver is powerful. Nothing else but it could have done this."

"But what if there's more than one nymph still out there?" The advisor shuddered. "You fought them to near extinction, long ago, but…what if one escaped? What if there's another nymph still alive?"

The king stood, his chair screeching back and red robe rippling. "You think I would be so careless as to let that happen?"

The advisor stumbled in his haste to step backwards. "N-no, Your Majesty. Certainly not. Forgive my stupidity. I shall go and send the order for Madnes Hatter and his companions' arrest." He used the excuse to exit the room, stumbling again.

"Dead or alive," the king's voice followed, "I want them."

Madnes kept a hand firmly on his hat, battling against the wind that was determined to rip it off, as they rode on dragon Pelur over Wonderland's landscape.

Oz had stayed behind, choosing his responsibility to the other crowv villages still in danger—to free them of the killing fungus and lead them to the safety of the duchess's palace. But not before declaring that he would be back, in what almost sounded like a threat. Madnes had to promise again and again that if they found the crowv woman inside one of the crystals, they wouldn't destroy it until Oz was there.

'How do I get myself into these situations? Seriously, this job is getting crazier and crazier,' thought Madness.

"This is an absurd plan, Madnes!" For the fifth time Cheshire grumbled through his whiskers. "Me form a team with that—*that*—wannabe cowboy?" Cheshire darted a glare at Cosmic Hunter.

"It's bounty hunter, cat. Get it straight," Cosmic grunted without looking.

"Don't call me cat!" Cheshire hissed. "Madnes, I should be with you, on *your* team. I'm your mentor. You'll need me!"

Madnes wanted to cover his ears from all the bickering. "I've made it on my own for some time now," he assured Cheshire once more. "I'll be fine. But you and Uncle Cosmic are taking on a dangerous quest; your assigned crystal is in the most difficult place. You'll need each other to get this done, and you two are the toughest and smartest of the group. Unless you really want Harrey or Alice to—"

"No, no, stop it. You know I'd never allow weak humans to go to such a dangerous place." Cheshire huffed. "Your reasoning makes sense, but that does not mean I have to like it."

Pelur rumbled, and the scales beneath their seats tremored. Cosmic craned his neck to peer over the dragon's side and grinned. "Our stop is here, he says! Do we need our tickets stamped?"

The one giant eye of Pelur's that they could see stared blankly at him, not getting the joke.

Rows of smoking mountains and charred terrain lay far below them, streaked with rivers of strange colors.

"Lovely place to hide a crystal…" Madnes frowned.

"Sure is!" Cosmic positioned himself near the dragon's right wing. "Ready to go, feline?"

"Once we land, yes." Cheshire crossed his furry arms. "Why? What are you thinking of—?"

Cosmic snatched up the cat with one arm and leaped off the dragon.

Madnes watched wide-eyed as they plummeted— Cheshire screeching like a banshee, claws digging in the man's skin.

Something like a parachute ballooned out then, slowing their fall.

"Of all the idiot, no-good…!" Cheshire's furious voice faded.

Sweatdrops beaded Madnes's forehead and he exhaled shakily, leaning back. Maybe pairing those two hadn't been such a smart idea, after all?

Dragon Pelur veered through the air, heading toward the next drop-off location.

"Wow. Uh, just so you know, I don't have a cool parachute with me, so I'll die if I do that," commented Harrey.

"You won't need one," rumbled Pelur.

In twenty minutes, they arrived at the next stop, rising into a sky of floating islands. Harrey gaped, mesmerized by the many networks of bridges that connected the airborne country.

Pelur held up his huge paw for Harrey and young Ash and Drisel to climb on; he then lowered them to the nearest buoyant green island. They hopped to the grass and waved back.

"Be careful, Harrey. I mean it!" Madnes shouted after them and waved as Pelur carried him and Alice back down under the clouds. "Keep those kids in your sight at all times!"

Once they'd lowered to the mainland, Alice flashed a smirk his way. "Of all people, you left them with Harrey?"

"Eh, he wasn't the ideal choice," Madnes admitted. "But I think those kids need a break from us and a chance to explore a little. The floating islands seemed like a safer option, and rather cool, if you ask me. I'm kind of jealous we couldn't take that mission."

"Saving the tough ones for us, hm?"

"I hope we're not biting off more than we can chew." He gave a faint laugh.

The wind battered his hat as the dragon descended to their final destination.

The story continues in…
Madness Solver in Wonderland 2

MADNESS
SOLVER
IN
WONDERLAND
2

EE RAWLS

THANK YOU

Thank you for reading! It was because of a writing prompt that this story came to be. I was a participant in the Blog Battle writing challenges, hosted by Rachael Ritchey, and the word prompt for that day was "madness." Now, when I think of that word, I just can't help but think of the Mad Hatter, right? And so, I began drafting this story about my wiser version of him, Madnes Hatter, and things took off from there!

If you loved Madness Solver in Wonderland and want to share it with other readers, please consider leaving an honest review on Amazon and Goodreads. This makes a huge difference for indie authors like me!

You can be the first to learn about new releases, extra content and book sales by signing up for my newsletter at:

eerawls.com

A huge thank you to Rachael and all my Blog Battle buddies, for their encouraging words and input as I crafted this tale! And thank you to all who read the story and quickly became fans—I loved reading your comments! Above all, thanks be to God, who makes me able.

Dive into a new series of adventure, monsters and elemental powers…

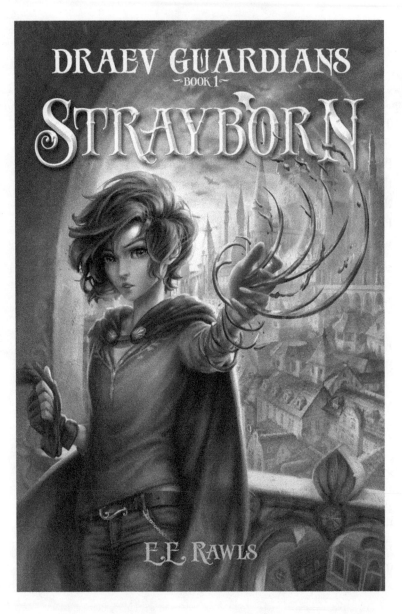

Available wherever books are sold, plus you can request it from your local library or bookstore!
Visit: www.eerawls.com

OTHER BOOKS

THE ALTEREDVERSE

Books in the *Alteredverse* are standalone tales that take place in our world, at different points in time, and they often feature the humanoid Altered Ones (read **Portal to Eartha** for the origin story of the Altered).

They can be read in any order. Some books take place during our time, and some far into the future. To see the full Timeline of events, and where each book fits, visit:

eerawls.com/alteredverse

If you enjoyed the world of *Madness Solver*, be sure to check out the other books in the *Alteredverse*. Also, check out the series **Draev Guardians** that takes place in the *Earthaverse* — the twin planet to our world (it can be read at any time and separately from *Alteredverse* books).

Recommended reading order:

- *Portal to Eartha*
- *Beast of the Night*
- *Madness Solver in Wonderland*

Portal to Eartha

Future Japan.
A clue to a secret portal world.
The only hope for Lotus, an Altered girl with the gift of
Healing, on the run from the mafia…

Beast of the Night

A one-armed, practical girl. A rude lord hiding a curse. A dark
secret with the town's fate hanging in the balance…

A Beauty and the Beast retelling with an Austrian twist and a
new breed of curse.

FROST

COMING SOON

How You Can

Help:

Reviews help boost a book on retailer websites so that it'll be found by more readers, which in turn helps support the author. Would you please leave a review at Amazon and Goodreads? It doesn't have to be much, just click on how many stars you want to rate the book, and maybe add a sentence or two on your thoughts.

E.E. Rawls is the product of a traveling family, who even lived in Italy for 6 years. She loves exploring the unknown, whether it be in a forest, the ruins of a forgotten castle, or in the pages of a book. Her brain runs on coffee, cuddly cats, and the mysterious beauty of nature while she writes.

Visit her online at **eerawls.com** and join her newsletter for updates and extra content, and get the FREE Draev Guardians short story:

STORM & CHOICE

CPSIA information can be obtained
at www.ICGtesting.com
Printed in the USA
BVHW030950140521
607265BV00007B/226